Praise for *Street*

★ "A compelling, morally challenging, and emotionally rewarding work . . . With skilled characterization, tight plotting, and a sensitive ear for the language of the streets, *Street Pharm* is a remarkable achievement."

&Quire, starred review

"A surprisingly hopeful book, one that respectfully acknowledges the intelligence and street smarts necessary for success, whether the challenge is drug dealing or college preparation."

—*Booklist*

"*Street Pharm* pierces through the 'glamour' and exposes the underbelly: the perils of hard drugs . . . Van Diepen's keen eye and ear . . . captures the social, physical and emotional costs of a young drug lord trying to keep it together in an unsettling urban landscape."

—*The Globe and Mail*

★★★★ "This book, set in inner-city Brooklyn, pushes the envelope of edgy writing for teens . . . it's gritty, the slang rings true and the story is not pretty. Maybe that's why it works."

—*Romantic Times*, 4 stars

Also by Allison van Diepen

Street Pharm

A 2007 ALA Top Ten Quick Pick for Reluctant Readers
A NYPL Book for the Teen Age

Snitch

Allison van Diepen

Simon Pulse
New York London Toronto Sydney

SIMON PULSE

An imprint of Simon & Schuster Children's Publishing Division

1230 Avenue of the Americas, New York, NY 10020

Copyright © 2007 by Allison van Diepen

All rights reserved, including the right of reproduction in

whole or in part in any form.

SIMON PULSE and colophon are registered trademarks of Simon & Schuster, Inc.

Designed by Sammy J. Yuen Jr.

The text of this book was set in Electra LH.

Manufactured in the United States of America

First Simon Pulse edition November 2007

10 9

Library of Congress Control Number 2007927645

ISBN-13: 978-1-4169-5030-1

ISBN-10: 1-4169-5030-3

For my parents

Thanks to the students who told me what I needed to know to write this book. You know who you are. And to my agent, Ashley Grayson, and my editor at Simon Pulse, Sangeeta Mehta, for their encouragement and assistance along the way.

NOTE TO READERS

All errors, inconsistencies and out-and-out screwups are purely the fault of my agent, editor, publisher, and anyone else who messed with my book before it made it into your hands. This is my story, and I'm gonna tell it like it happened.

THE DEAN'S OFFICE

"People always make it sound like God is a man. But we've got no proof of that."

Everybody gasped. Then a few snickers and giggles.

I felt myself blush, but I hurried on. "The whole idea of God looking like a man is a European concept. Back in Ancient Greece—"

"You saying God is a girl?" Eddie Evans shouted. "So God's got titties and a—"

The class erupted in laughter.

I kicked my volume up. "No, that's *not* what I'm saying. God is not male or female."

"So God is a transvestite?" Jay shouted from the back row.

"Not a transvestite, dumbass, a hermaphrodite," Cassie said. "That's when you got a package *and* a coochie."

Ms. Howard's face reddened. I didn't know if she was going to pass out or go postal. She yelled at everyone to settle down, but no one paid attention. She turned on me. "Just hand in your paper and sit down. We've heard enough."

"You're not gonna let me present it? I spent a lot of time on this."

"Too bad you didn't choose a more appropriate topic."

"But this was one of the choices you gave us! It was topic seven—*explore how different cultures*—"

"Sit down," she snapped.

Knowing when to shut up wasn't usually a problem for me, but I heard myself saying, "This isn't fair. *You're* the one who assigned the topic."

The class went, "Ooooooohhhhh."

"Go to the dean, Julia."

The class was so quiet, you could hear a pin drop. As everybody watched, I picked up my books and stalked out. You really should have seen her face. She didn't think that A-student Julia DiVino would dare stand up to her.

My legs felt like jelly, probably more from the stress of the situation than anything else. Dad was going to kick my ass if he had to take off work to go to a suspension hearing. Or would he be proud that I stuck to my guns? I doubted it.

I surprised myself by heading toward the bathroom on my way to the dean's office. I guess I needed a few minutes to let the redness in my cheeks go down.

Everybody knew Diana the bathroom lady. She was in her forties, with bleached blonde hair and heavy-metal tattoos. Her job was to spend her entire day outside the girls' bathroom making sure nothing nasty was happening—no drugs, no fights . . . no suicides.

"Hey there, baby." Diana reached out to receive my bathroom pass but I shook my head.

"I don't have one."

"Why not?"

"I've been sent to the dean's office by Ms. Howard but I want a minute to . . ."

"Go ahead, sweetie."

Our bathrooms were like a mini Brooklyn housing project, littered with trash and covered in graffiti. The graffiti was mostly gang stuff: *RLB rock da house, Hermanas Mexicalis is bad bitches, Crab girls got crabs*. The worst culprits were the school's biggest girl gang, the RLB, aka the Real Live Bitches. I'd spent lots of toilet-sittings deciphering their codes. All you needed to know was a little pig Latin and a little Creole and you could crack pretty much any code.

I splashed cold water on my face and let it spike my lashes and dribble into my eyes. The shock of the water made me feel a bit better. I patted my face dry with scraping brown paper towels, careful not to smear my (thankfully waterproof) mascara. Running my fingers through my hair, I headed out to face the dean, thanking Diana as I left.

"Holla back!"

I jumped when I heard the voice behind me. Turned out it was Black Chuck. "Chuck, what up?"

"I told you, don't call me Chuck. I'm going by Black now."

"What kind of a name is Black?"

"My kind of name, *Ju*."

I rolled my eyes. "I told you not to call me that. Everybody's going to think I'm Jewish."

"So? Nothing wrong with that, is there?"

"'Course not, but—"

"No butts. Only asses. So where we going, Ju? Don't tell me you cutting. Not Miss DiVino. You got a sub in Howard's class?"

"Actually, she sent me to see the dean."

"Yeah, right."

"I'm serious. It's because I said in my speech that God wasn't a man and didn't have a package. She got upset."

Black Chuck burst out laughing. "I got you. Well, if they gonna suspend your ass, I'll walk you down there."

"You're so sweet."

He dropped me off outside the office. As he walked away, I shouted over my shoulder, "Your pants are falling down."

He shouted back, "Damn right they are!"

The dean's office was a large space with about a dozen orange plastic chairs and several connecting rooms. It used to be guidance central, but the admin switched the offices when it realized that more students needed suspensions than programming advice.

I'd always felt sorry for the poor suckers who got sent here. Today I was one of them, along with a hot Hispanic guy who sat outside Dean Hallett's door.

The guy lifted his eyes, meeting mine. I looked away quickly, sitting down two seats away from him. I felt him giving me a once-over before looking back down at his MP3.

Just my luck, Hallett was on duty today. She was the strictest of the deans. I took a deep breath, wondering what she'd do to me.

The guy didn't seem worried. He was nodding his head to his music.

"Is it too loud?" he asked, removing one of his earphones.

"No, it's fine," I said, without looking at him.

I was hoping he'd put the earphone back in and go back to minding his business, but he kept looking at me. "So, you in trouble or something?"

"Well, I *am* in the dean's office."

"That doesn't mean anything. I'm just here to get my ID card." I glanced at him. His smile was smooth, easy.

"Not me, unfortunately."

"I feel you. I've been at the dean's office myself a few times at my old school."

Okay, so I had to ask. "What school's that?"

"You wouldn't know it unless you know Detroit."

"Detroit, huh? I hear that place is gangsta. Guess you won't have trouble getting used to Brooklyn."

"No trouble at all."

"How'd you end up in Brooklyn?"

But he couldn't answer, because that's when Hallett's door opened. She was a heavyset woman who looked at you like you were a suspect, kind of like S. Epatha Merkerson on *Law and Order*.

"Hi, Eric, come on in." Her eyes landed on me. "Was there something I could help you with, Julia?"

"Uh, well . . . Ms. Howard wanted me to speak to you."

"All right. I'll see you in a few minutes." She let him into her office and closed the door.

I sighed. Wait until she found out why I was there.

Q

My best friend, Q, begged for the 411 on the bus ride home. She already knew about my trip to the dean's office, and that I'd been spotted talking to a hot guy.

We took the special bus that stopped outside the school. It was convenient, and we both knew it wasn't smart to hang out at the bus stops on Nostrand Avenue. There was always drama going on, and we didn't want to be part of it.

"You've got to be kidding. Not *literally* one minute."

"I'm serious. One and a half, tops. I told her what happened and she said to try to be less controversial next time so Ms. Howard won't get upset. That's it."

"She must like you."

"She likes *us*." I smiled. "'Cause we're cornballs."

Q laughed. We weren't cornball Honors students, but we weren't totally mainstream either. We fit somewhere between the gangbangers and the nerds, though we weren't really sure where.

In a school run by gangs, staying out was harder than joining. But Q and me made a pact in seventh grade not to join any gang, and we stuck to it. There were a few different gangs represented at the school: Real Live Bitches and Real Live Niggaz (Blood connection), Hands Up (Blood connection), Sixty-Six Mafia (Crip connection), Flatbush Junction Crips (Crip connection.) We knew who our friends were, and were careful about what we said. If people thought we were haters, it would only be a matter of time before we got jumped.

Q had mocha skin and a wide, mobile mouth. She had a great figure, petite but with boobs, which got her mad attention. Her skin was good too, despite the occasional zit in her T-zone.

Q's name was actually Latisha Stairs, but over the years it went from Latisha to Queen Latifa to Queen and now, just Q.

"Wanna come over?" Asking her was a daily ritual. Unless she had dance class, she came over to my place for a couple of hours pretty much every weekday. I liked the company, and she liked the downtime when she didn't have to deal with her mom or her annoying younger brother and sister.

Q always had to be home for dinner at 5:30 p.m. on the dot or her mom would go into her speech about young people not respecting their parents. The lecture was the same every time with little variations she'd picked up like "You should've seen that mama backhand her child in the grocery store—you be glad I ain't taking to you like that," or "Her child missed dinner one night, and she was pregnant and not a day above fourteen. *Fourteen*, do you hear me?"

Yeah, that was Q's mom. Her dad was a firefighter in the city, but since her parents were divorced, she only saw him every month or two.

We got off the number 44 at the corner of Nostrand and Flatbush, and jaywalked to my apartment building opposite the projects. On bleak days, it looked gray and depressing as hell. Today, with the September sun gleaming off the brick, I was almost proud of where I lived. Most of my friends lived in much worse.

I dug into my jeans and fished out my key.

The DiVino crib was pretty stylin', with a black leather couch and love seat, an oval glass coffee table, cream carpeting, and an entertainment system, to which my dad had added a flat-screen TV a few months back. By the front window was a desk with a computer. Dad thought I needed the most up-to-date technology to do my homework; he didn't know that I spent most of my computer time IM'ing my friends and watching YouTube.

Q had barely entered the crib and found the Doritos when she asked me to tell her more about the guy in the office.

"His name's Eric. He's from Detroit. That's all I know." I chose not to mention that I wasn't exactly sweet to him right off the bat. Q thought I self-sabotaged when in the vicinity of good-looking guys.

"Is he a junior?"

"I don't know. He looks more like a senior."

"Well, you'll have to find a way to talk to him again. Maybe he'll be at the dance Friday night. I hear he's so fine." Her eyebrows went up and down. "Mmmm . . ."

"As if! Don't look at me like that."

"Let me guess, he ain't your type?"

"Right."

"You always say that, Julia. Chill. Not every guy's like Joe."

I stared at her. She knew not to bring him up. She knew

mentioning that asshole could put me in a bad mood for the rest of the day. She just didn't know the whole story.

"Sorry, Julia." She licked the powdered cheese off her fingertips. "I'm just saying. It's time you made an effort to find a guy."

"I'm not *not* making an effort."

"Good. So you cannot *not* make an effort Friday night at the dance."

"Maybe I will. Maybe I won't."

Q crunched some more, grinning.

Tony DiVino, aka My Dad

I was the devil's daughter. My Italian grandma told me that once and ever since I liked the idea.

"I had-a three sons," she told me one sweaty summer night on their porch in Astoria, Queens. "One was a chef, one was a cab driver, and one was a devil. Don'tcha be asking me which one your papa was!"

I gave my most wicked grin as she eyed me above her reading glasses. She seemed to think I took after my dad. But I also knew that she was proud of her youngest son ever since he started operating subways for the MTA.

Tony DiVino had been getting into scrapes since he was in the cradle. The worst one was marrying my mom, Marisol, the daughter of Puerto Rican immigrants. I'd heard enough

of my grandma's mutterings to know what she thought of His-
panics. Gold diggers, hustlers, shoplifters, all of them.

I'd always hurt for my mom because I knew how they
must've treated her. It was just stupid for the DiVinos to think
that she married my dad for any reason but love. When she
married him he was stocking shelves in a grocery store. Even
a dumbass gold digger could've done better than that. If it was
money she wanted, she probably would've encouraged him
to become a pusher instead of a subway operator.

I looked up from my food to the picture of my mom on
the mantle. That picture had smiled down at me almost as
far back as I could remember. She'd died in a car accident
when I was six, and I only remembered what she looked
like from pictures. But I remembered how she smelled.
Sometimes I caught her scent out of the blue—on the
street, at the mall, at home. And I'd remember how it felt
to be in her arms.

The door opened, jolting me from my thoughts. "Dad?"

"Hey, bella." Dad carried a pizza. He looked down at the
cheese-smeared bowl on the coffee table. "You've already
eaten? But I brought pepperoni pizza from Angelo's!"

How should I know he was going to do that? I was surprised enough that he was actually home. But I didn't bother

saying it, because Dad was never going to change. The man obviously had adult ADD. Most of what I said went in one ear and out the other.

"Mac and cheese again?" He frowned.

"I didn't get a chance to go for groceries." Usually I cooked myself something good. Q said I made an amazing stir-fry. "It doesn't matter, I'm still hungry. I can have a slice of pizza. Maybe two."

I promised myself I'd eat at least one and a half slices. Sure, I was already pretty full, but it wasn't often Dad came home with a surprise like this. I had to make him feel it was worth it if he was ever going to do it again.

Dad went to change. I put out a couple of plates, then got him a beer and opened it with the bottle opener on his key chain.

When he came back he wore an old Yankees shirt and jeans. He once told me that the biggest division between the MTA employees wasn't black or white, male or female, but Mets or Yankees. I wasn't into baseball myself, though I had great memories of going to games with my dad when I was young. And I tried to stay up on the scores in case he asked for my opinion on the games. I wanted him to think that I watched baseball when he wasn't around.

When he wasn't working, Dad was out with his buddies or his girl, Gina, a thirty-five-year-old secretary in a real estate office. She reminded me of Paula Abdul—short, done-up, and the kind of sweet that made your teeth ache. They'd been going out for five or six months, but I'd only seen her a few times. I knew it didn't matter, because with Dad it never lasted more than a few months. Which meant there was no point in anybody making too much of an effort.

Dad had a dark, scruffy Benicio Del Toro look that seemed to go over well with the ladies despite a few extra pounds. And of course, he had his God-given (as he put it) Italian charm.

"I'm going to the dance at South Bay Friday night," I said. Dad usually didn't remember those things, but I figured I'd tell him anyway.

"Have fun. Don't forget to wear a bulletproof vest."

I rolled my eyes. "It's not *that* bad."

"Since when is a shooting in the locker room *not that bad?*"

Okay, despite his adult ADD, Dad remembered some things. "That was two years ago, Dad."

"So whoever did it got arrested and charged, right?" When I shook my head, he said, "Exactly. It's a lawless culture these days."

"Yeah, well, the kid didn't die, thankfully."

"That's comforting. Forgive me if I can't wait till you get out of that shithole school." He licked the tomato sauce off his fingers. "Pardon my French."

GEOGRAPHY OF MY LIFE: ASTORIA,FLATBUSH, AND SOUTH BAY

Before moving to Flatbush ten years ago, we lived in Astoria, Queens. Dad and I moved down here so that he could be closer to his job. He drove the 5 train from Brooklyn College to the Bronx and back about a million times a day.

Now I lived on the border between the projects of Flatbush and the leafy neighborhood of Midwood (or Victorian Flatbush as white people call it.) At first nobody was sure what to think of the Hispanic/Italian kid from Queens. But eventually I was welcomed in, and my second favorite food after pizza became Jamaican patties.

Like a million other teenagers, I'm bused to a school that isn't in my neighborhood so that I can have *better educational opportunities*. I applied to South Bay because it had some law-focused courses that I thought would look good on a college application. Too bad the school's going downhill fast. Last year it was ranked the fifth-most dangerous school in all five boroughs.

Though most of the students at my school are black and Hispanic, most of the staff is white. There's not a lot of exciting stuff in this neighborhood: McDonald's, libraries, delis, little men in yarmulkes muttering in Yiddish on street corners looking to catch a bus or their wives cavorting with gentiles. Best of all, it's a change from Flatbush, where sirens and gunfire keep me up late at night worrying. Worrying that one of my friends will get shot. Worrying that my dad isn't going to get home safe.

The Dance

Friday night. Me and my girls, Q, Marie, Vicky, and Melisha, arrived at the dance twenty minutes after it started. Screw being fashionably late—we wanted to go through security as fast as possible so we could hit the dance floor.

Or, as Marie said, we wanted first pick of the ass.

We'd been a group since junior high, when the five of us ended up in the same class. Q, Melisha, and me already knew one another. Vicky and Marie were newbies from other schools and sticking together. It actually started with a school yard beef; word got to Marie that Q had made fun of her hairstyle in front of some guys. Instead of letting my best friend get jumped, which I heard was the plan, I went to Marie and Vicky to plead Q's innocence. They not only believed me, they gave me props for going up to them and went over to meet Q and Melisha. We'd all been tight ever since. To this day, Q says she never said that about Marie's hair, but knowing Q's views on the importance of good hair, I never believed her.

It's amazing how we all stuck like glue, especially considering Marie was a member of the Real Live Bitches. She got recruited in freshman year, when the RLB was scrambling to counter floods of Crips coming in. They'd tried to recruit all of us that year, but we made them back off by playing innocent and weak, qualities the RLB hated. Marie was the one who got up in their faces, and after fighting some members, she decided to stop resisting her destiny and become a Bitch herself.

Unlike most of the RLB, Marie still hung out with nonmembers whenever she felt like it. In fact, she told me once that the main reason she joined was for a shot at some hot guys. You see, she was mad horny.

To my surprise, the gym was crowded when we walked in. Probably with freshmen, but I didn't care. At least there were people on the dance floor. We hit it immediately, cheesy colorful lights flashing around us.

The music wasn't half bad for a school-hired DJ, though we only heard the clean versions of songs, like Akon's ode to strippers, "I Wanna Love You." We sang along using the real lyrics, and had a good laugh dancing with imaginary stripper poles.

Within an hour the gym filled to the max, and I couldn't help scanning for Eric, cute dean's office guy. I'd promised myself that if he showed up, I'd make a point of talking to him, if only to prove to Q that I wasn't a punk.

I didn't see him. What I saw instead was a bunch of kids displaying gang colors, mostly flags and bandannas they'd smuggled in. I looked at my watch, wondering how much dancing we'd get in before trouble started.

When the DJ got on the mike to do shout-outs, I walked off the dance floor to take a breather and a drink at the fountain. As soon as I caught my breath and reapplied my lip gloss, I'd go back to my friends.

"Hey, I know you," someone shouted in my ear.

He materialized at my elbow, like out of nowhere. He seemed bigger than I remembered, maybe because he wasn't hunched in a chair. Six feet tall at least, with broad shoulders filling out his Pistons jersey. Sean John jeans hung loosely around his legs, held up by a belt with a silver buckle.

I felt a smile coming, but I kept it subtle—no way I was going to let on that I'd been hoping to see him here.

"I know you too. . . ." I said as if I didn't remember his name.

"It's Eric Valienté."

"Julia DiVino."

He leaned closer. "Di-what?"

"*DiVino*. It's Italian. But I'm Puerto Rican on my mom's side."

He smiled. "I didn't know I was messing with no Puerto Rican." He rolled his Rs like he spoke Spanish. Sexy.

I could hear my heartbeat, separate from the music, pounding in my ears. Eric Valienté was giving me sensory overload. We had to stand really close to talk over the loud music, and it was messing with my hormones.

"I'm a mutt too," he said. "Dad's Dominican, Mom's Mexican."

"Nice mix."

"They didn't think so. They got divorced."

That could be a conversation killer if I didn't keep the ball rolling. "I never heard how you ended up in Brooklyn."

"Got into some trouble in Detroit. Nothing big, but my mom thought I should come here for a fresh start. So I'm living with my dad now. How's that for an answer?"

"Okay, except you didn't say what the trouble was."

"Right, I didn't." He winked, then turned his attention to the dance floor.

Shit. Had I said the wrong thing? Did he think I wasn't good-looking from up close? My dad hadn't thought one crooked eyetooth justified the cost of braces. Probably true, but I cursed him for it anyway. Plus, my skin was giving me problems. I'd dropped ten bucks on oil-free cover-up, and I hoped it was working.

"Are all the teachers here crazy like that one?" he asked.

I spotted Ms. Carter doing some disco moves in the middle of a group of kids. The moves actually went well with the Usher song playing. "Ah, she's just having fun. She's the least crazy teacher you'll find here."

"You playing?"

"I don't play."

He smiled. Yeah, we were feeling each other. I wondered what he'd do if I leaned over and kissed him. Of course, I wouldn't do that. Not unless I were drunk, which I wasn't, unfortunately.

Then somebody grabbed my sleeve.

"Who is *he*?" It was my friend Melisha, her eyelids sparkling with silver glitter.

"I'll tell you later. Now bounce, okay?"

"Fine, but I hope he got friends for the rest of us!"

I turned back to Eric. He was scanning the room. "Lot of people rocking colors," he said.

I sighed. "Yeah. It's mostly a Blood school, but we've got more and more Crips here now. When they closed down Tilson, lots of them came here."

He nudged his chin toward the Crips. "You see what they're doing?"

I saw. There was a group of Crips by the speakers. Two of them were doing the *CripWalk*—a little dance meant to piss off the Bloods.

"Can't they keep that shit out of here?" I looked around, spotting the security guards. They weren't paying any attention. They were flirting with some girls.

"I think something's gonna start," he said. "We better—"

I stopped listening. I watched a guy in a red do-rag walk up to one of the Crip dancers and snuff him right in the face.

Chaos broke out.

I felt Eric grab my arm and drag me through the crowd. Half the people in the gym were running toward the fight, half were running away from it to the main doors. I covered my face against the long nails and elbows as Eric yanked me through the mess of people.

I felt him push me against the wall. But it wasn't a wall, it was a door. It must've been a fire exit. I found myself in the parking lot behind the school. A bunch of kids rushed out after us.

"What the hell is happening?" I tried to catch my breath.

"They're trying to kill each other," he said. "Nothing new. I gotta go."

"Don't!" I grabbed his arm, but he pulled away and disappeared back inside.

Why the hell did he go back in? What was he thinking?

"God, Julia!" Q threw her arms around me. "I was worried you were caught in the middle of that! Somebody got stabbed. Did you see what happened?"

"Bloods and Crips," I said. "That's what happened."

ALL TALK

"Julia's got beef with gangs," Melisha said, stuffing a forkful of chicken soo guy into her mouth. Skinny, leggy, five eleven, that girl could eat anything, and did. "Damn gangs stopped her from getting some action with that guy."

We'd snagged a table in the window of a Chinese take-out halfway between the school and the subway station. The place and surrounding sidewalk were packed with kids from the dance who weren't ready to call it a night after the drama. We were all here but Marie, who'd ditched us for her RLB friends.

"His name is Eric Valienté." I couldn't help but empha-size the sexy last name. "And I doubt there would've been any action."

Q scoffed. "He was practically all over you."

"Yeah, yeah." *I wish.*

"Don't be all guy-cynical," Melisha said. "Forget about Joe. He didn't know what he had."

"Thanks, but I really don't need a pep talk."

"I think you do, Julia. We need to get you a new boyfriend so we can have access to his crew. Joe never lived up to his promise to hook the rest of us up, that bastard. Did Eric have friends with him?"

"Not that I saw," I said.

"He's new, maybe he doesn't have friends yet," Vicky said. She was a short, chubby redhead—the Irish version of Marie—but much less mouthy. "I wonder what gang he'll join."

"Maybe he won't join a gang," I said. "Maybe that kind of drama doesn't turn him on."

"I hear that." Q slapped me five.

"Well, we can all say good-bye to dances for the rest of the year," Vicky told us. "Ms. Miklovic said if we had another incident, she'd cancel them all."

"That's bullshit," Q said. "It's not our fault. They should kick out the gangbangers."

"That would mean half the school," Vicky said.

"What about prom next year?" Melisha looked horrified. "You don't think they'll cancel it, do you?"

"There's a first for everything," I said.

I came home to the sounds of dance music and chatter. The place was empty, of course, but I usually left the radio and living room light on, because I hated coming home to a quiet, dark apartment—and because the only thing worse than an empty apartment was one with a burglar in it.

Dad spent most Friday and Saturday nights at Gina's place in Bensonhurst. This weekend he'd taken her to Atlantic City. He said he liked it because of the fancy but affordable hotel rooms, the shows, and of course, the gambling. I thought he liked it because, since I wasn't old enough to gamble, he had an excuse not to take me along.

Not that I wanted to spend a weekend with him and Gina, but still.

I changed into my pjs, a soft, worn tee and cotton shorts, and settled on the couch, flicking channels. I caught the tail end of a show with two middle-aged British ladies exploring a haunted house and urging the spirits on to the light. It was cool. I'm sure they, unlike my sociology class, would have appreciated my research paper.

I thought of Eric Valienté and wondered what he would think. Whether he agreed with me or not, it would be cool if he at least had an opinion. Maybe that should be my way of figuring out guys from now on—ask them a tough question and see what they say.

If I'd asked Joe his view on religion, he probably would have said that he liked the idea of multiple wives. Maybe that would have woken me up in time.

I'd met Joe in the crush of people on the Fourth of July. Somehow he and his group latched on to me and my friends, and by the end of the night, I'd let him kiss me and tuck his hand into the ass pocket of my jeans.

An Italian jock, Joe was a senior at Jamaica High School. We'd dated for a month and I ended up, stupidly, giving up my virginity a few days before he dropped me. He claimed it was obvious the whole time that he wasn't looking for a relationship. Bullshit. Joe had done everything he could to reel me in. And I'd walked right into that player's cage.

I hadn't told Q or the girls what really happened between us. Way too humiliating. Even now, the thought of him made my stomach turn.

Thank God Joe lived in Queens, where I didn't have to see his dumb "What'd I do?" face.

Screw him. It was way past time to forget about that loser.

I wondered if I'd get a chance to talk to Eric again. Would he really have asked for my number? Too many guys were all talk, no follow-through. They'll ask for your number at a party and never call.

All I knew was, I was damned bitter that the gang members at my school had ruined my chance to talk to him more. It wasn't every day a new hottie showed up at South Bay—at least, not one who wasn't already owned by a gang.

Truth was, it was mad rare.

THE TRUTH ABOUT MY TEACHERS

Third week of school, junior year. By then I had my teachers figured out.

Ms. Howard, Sociology/Anthropology: Uptight because she didn't have a sex life.

Mr. Finklestein, Economics: Probably tried to be a stand-up comic when he was young, but got booed off the stage. Now he punished future generations by forcing us to listen to his stupid jokes.

Ms. Russo, Modern Dance: Wild twenty-something who refused to grow up. She got bitchy when she was hungover from clubbing with her friends.

Mr. McLennan, Math: Miserable teacher who'd been

hoping his whole life to switch to the phys ed department. Fat chance, with his gut.

Mr. Greenwood, Earth Science: Teaching was good—he could be back on Long Island by 2:30 p.m. and on the golf course by 3 p.m.

And then there was *Ms. Ivey, American History*: New to Brooklyn and fresh out of college, she was young and eager, and I liked that. I knew early on that she'd be my fave this year, if only because I felt sorry for her. Everybody was already giving her a hard time. She was just too priss for us to take seriously.

Poor Ms. Ivey. I'd lay concrete in a heat wave before I'd become a teacher.

At least cops got danger pay.

I was mad surprised when Eric Valienté ended up in Ms. Ivey's period 6 class. He walked in after the late bell, showed her his program, and chose the free seat *right behind me*.

"Hi, Julia." He gave my shoulder a little squeeze and slid into his seat.

"Hey."

Of all the free seats to choose! (I hoped my hair looked

okay from the back.) I couldn't help smiling. But I wiped it away as soon as I felt the glares of the Real Live Bitches—they had obviously noticed the new guy.

Well, he was fair game. And they'd find out soon that he wasn't going to join the Real Live Niggaz. I didn't know it for sure, but my instincts told me that Eric was too smart for that.

He tapped my shoulder. "Got any paper?"

"Sure."

Damn, he looked amazing in ice-blue Rocawear.

I turned my attention to Ms. Ivey, who was starting the lesson. I took some notes.

I felt a tap on my arm, and a small, folded note appeared over my shoulder. I took it and read it.

I thought my school back in Detroit was wack but this school is WILDIN' OUT. Peeps are smoking weed in the stairwell!

I wrote back: *This school is messed up, no doubt. I'm just trying to get my credits so I can get the hell out of here. How are your classes?*

He wrote: *They already changed my schedule twice. Does Ivey give a lot of homework?*

I wrote: *No. Just come to class and be nice and you'll be fine.*

He wrote: *What does being nice got to do with it?*

I wrote: *Because lots of people are disrespecting her. If you don't, she'll love you and pass you. Trust me.*

He wrote: *Then that's what I'll do.*

I wrote: *I knew you were a smart guy.* Then I drew a little happy face.

AFTER SCHOOL AT THE SHARK TANK

Me and my girls decided to stick around after school to join the crowd watching the football tryouts. Every year the South Bay Sharks were getting closer and closer to making the city finals. And, according to our stats, the players were getting hotter and hotter.

"*Who is dat?*" Marie exclaimed, pointing to a six-footer on the defensive line. "Does he pad his ass or what?"

Marie loved a good butt. Her own was round and wide, and she swung it in just the right way to get a guy's attention.

Beside her, Melisha gulped her drink. "That ain't padding, that's some real man-ass. There's enough of that to share."

"If he's dishing it out, I'll have a slice," Vicky said.

We nodded in agreement as we checked out the other

players. Then we all groaned when a group of cheerleaders jogged onto the field. They put on a boom box and started practicing their stepping.

"They don't know how to move!" Marie jumped up and started swinging her butt around as we clapped to the beat of Chris Brown's latest. "C'mon!"

We stood up on the bleachers and started dancing, following Marie's lead. I wasn't embarrassed—everyone on the bleachers was saying or doing something stupid anyway.

I stopped dancing when I caught sight of a familiar figure walking below the bleachers. The warm sun glistened off his short, slightly curly black hair.

God, he was fine. He looked like Sean Paul, with his slow, sexy stride and sharp, dark features.

Eric saw me too. He waved for me to come down to talk to him.

I told the girls, "I'll be back in a sec," and walked down the bleachers.

"Hey," I said. "What up?"

"On my way to play some ball. What about you—trying out to be a cheerleader or something?"

"We were just having fun."

"I could see that," he said, restraining a smile.

"So, how's your first week been? Your teachers okay?"

"All teachers are weird. I don't get why anybody would spend their days in front of thirty kids who don't wanna be there."

"It's a power thing. You can't be the leader of your own country, so you get your own classroom. Mr. Greenwood always says, 'You can't join this nation's democracy until you're eighteen. Until then, I'm your dictator.'"

"Are you serious? I'm glad I don't have him. I can't stand that shit." He squinted at the basketball courts, where a group of guys was gathering. "I gotta go. How about giving me your number?"

My heart slammed against my ribs. Did I hear him right?

"Sorry, what?"

He smiled. "I ain't hitting on you. I just thought it'd be cool to talk sometime."

"Uh, sure. You got a pen?"

"Better." He took out his cell. "What's the number?"

I told him.

He typed in my name. "JULIA DIVINE." He clicked SAVE.

"Wait, it's DiVino, not Divine."

"I know." He winked at me. "Later."

BLACK CHUCK

About once a month me and Black Chuck went to our favorite restaurant for cheeseburgers. The place was owned by Arabs (A-raabs as most of us pronounced it) and had the best burgers in Flatbush. Two seventy-five for a thick, juicy quarter-pounder dripping with grease and American cheese. The best part was when the slop of grease and cheese piled in a blob on the side of my plate, and Chuck slurped it up with a straw.

Black Chuck's real name was Philip Charles, but I can't remember the last time anyone called him that. Even his teachers called him Chuck, though not Black.

Our friendship meant a lot to me. He was the one who took me under his wing when I first moved into the neighborhood, telling me which adults I could cry to if I skinned my knee and which to avoid like the plague. I'll never forget the first day he came up to me on the swings, small and bony with a nappy Afro, his tongue purple from the red-and-blue gumballs he was chewing. Guess the rest is history.

We didn't have a lot in common, I admit. I was a good student, and he barely made a blip on the attendance roster. Personally, I thought it was my influence that kept him from dropping out altogether. Okay, so maybe I was taking too much credit. Black Chuck loved to be in the center of things, and that meant he had to hang around the school. Too bad he was still technically a freshman when he should be a junior.

Over the years lots of people gossiped that something was going on between us. Lots of people were wrong. Sure, with his smooth chocolate-cupcake skin and knock-you-on-your-ass smile, Black Chuck was a fine-looking guy, but he was like a brother to me, and I knew he saw me as a sister.

Only one thing screwed up the picture: Black Chuck was a Crip. Being Crip was all he'd ever known, since his big brother, Scrap, was head of the Flatbush Junction Crips. But Black Chuck always said he hadn't joined just because of Scrap. He said the Crips were a family, a brotherhood, and the fact was, there was safety in numbers for a guy on the streets of Flatbush.

"I hear you getting freaky with some guy." He took another bite of his cheeseburger.

"Yeah, right." I sprinkled salt on my last few fries. "He's new to school and we're kind of friends. Barely even that."

"I heard you was shaking your booty for him yesterday at the football tryouts."

"*What?* Who told you that?"

He grinned as he sipped his Coke. "You testy today!"

"I'm not! Was it Marie who told you?" At his nod, I said, "She was just bullshitting you. She always does."

"Too bad. It sounded mad funny."

"Sorry to disappoint you. Are you going to Raoume's party tomorrow night?"

"I'll see."

That was another thing about Black Chuck. He never made plans in advance. He came knocking on my door when he wanted to hang. If I was doing homework and had to send him away, he never took it personally. Other times we chilled together, channel surfing or listening to some tunes on the radio. There was nothing like chilling with Black Chuck.

He yelled to the A-raab behind the counter. "Can you bring some more fries? My homegirl's out."

He was great like that too.

THE WRITERS' CLUB

The next day during my lunch period I went to a meeting of the Writers' Club. I went mainly because it would be a good extracurricular activity to put on my college application. Truth was, I never found the meetings anything but wack. They went something like this:

We start ten minutes late, waiting for Mr. Britt to show up and get his act together.

Spend fifteen minutes talking about where the club is going and what different things we can be doing and how we can get more kids interested.

Spend last fifteen minutes sharing bits of our work with the group as we all complain that there's never enough time.

Writing-wise, I was a snob. I didn't see how the other

members were qualified to critique my work. I mean, two of them ganged up on me last week, saying it was not grammatically correct to start a sentence with "and" or "but." "Look, this is a short story, not an essay," I said. "I can write as many ands and buts as I want."

But they didn't get it. Neither did Mr. Britt. Every year he wanted the club to put together a booklet of our work as if it would be a big deal to see our names in print. What Mr. Britt really wanted was something nice and shiny to show the principal.

As usual, he came in ten minutes late, apologized, and put down his overflowing briefcase. "Why don't we begin by taking a closer look at how to add some excitement to our club? Look, we have . . . seven people. How can we double that? Any ideas?"

More like, how can we get people to show up more than once? He must've forgotten that there'd been three times as many people at our first meeting. Boredom drove them away.

Vincent Baker's hand shot up. "Maybe if we held our meetings earlier in the week, more people would come."

Mr. Britt smoothed a hand over his jaw. "That's a possibility."

"What if we hold a contest?" Alya suggested.

He pointed at her. "I like it!"

"We could have a category for short stories and one for poetry," Alya said.

"But what could we give for prizes?" Mary asked. "We don't have any money."

"I could speak to the principal about that," Mr. Britt said. Any excuse to brag about his club. "All we'd need would be, say, fifty dollars for the winner of each category. Leave that to me. Now, what else can we do?"

I spent the rest of the meeting wondering what sort of poem I should submit to the contest. I had several decent ones at home to choose from. Maybe I'd write a new one.

I wondered if Eric would be impressed if I won. I'd sure as hell like to win. And by the looks of the other writers here, I had a good chance. Unless, of course, there were other good writers at this school who were smart enough to stay away from the Writers' Club.

The bell rang. I shoved the brown bag with the last of my lunch in the garbage and pushed through the crowds in order to make it to Russo's dance class on time.

I was so bent on getting to the gym that I didn't notice who was walking beside me until he nudged me. "In a hurry?"

It was Eric.

"Just trying to get to class without getting stomped on."

"Yeah, these halls are crazy. God, how many people are in this school? Ten thousand?"

"Closer to four thousand." I stopped walking. I had to turn right here, and I figured he was going left to where the classrooms were. "Time for dance class."

"I'll walk you there. Ms. Wharton's too blind to see if anyone comes in late anyway."

I couldn't believe he was actually offering to walk me to class. I wasn't going to argue.

Unfortunately, the gym was just around the next corner, so we didn't have a chance to say much. The door was wide open, and I knew the other girls could see that he'd walked me there. I could feel the mercury on my reputation meter rising.

Just as I was going to say "bye," he asked me, "Are you going to Raoume's party?"

"Yeah, I'm going. You?"

"Maybe. Where's it at again?"

"It's near my place. You should come with us." I tried to sound casual.

"Who are you going with? A bunch of girls, right?"

I sure as hell was going to get Black Chuck to come if it

meant Eric would go with us. "Probably my girl, Q, and my buddy, Black Chuck."

The late bell rang. Two more girls slipped past me into the gym before the door closed. But I couldn't go in before we figured this out.

"So, you'll come with us?" I asked.

"Sure. I'll call you at dinnertime and we'll make a plan."

"Great."

He walked away. I didn't imagine that, did I?

Why did he bother with me when every girl in the school wanted him? *Chill*, I told myself. He was new in school and I was easy to talk to. It didn't mean he wanted to *date* me.

I knocked on the gym door. Ms. Russo answered. "Some of the girls tell me that you're late because you've been standing out here *flirting*."

"Uh . . ."

"Well, since you're never late and your classmates tell me he's cute, I'll let it slide this once." I could see she was holding back a smile.

I dropped my bag at the side of the shiny hardwood floor and joined the girls lined up in front of the mirrors.

I felt icy stares coming from a trio of Real Live Bitches.

Eat your heart out, girls.

TONIGHT

For the rest of the day I could only think of one thing: Eric. Okay, two things: Eric and the party. Eric *at* the party. With me. Tonight.

A horrible thought occurred to me on the bus ride home from school. "What if he doesn't call?"

"Who cares?" Q said. "You're not into this guy, right?"

"Right." We both laughed.

"I bet he feels the same," she said. "I heard you were all over each other today outside Ms. Russo's class."

"Who said that?"

"Everyone. You're gaining status, girl. People are saying you snatched him up before any of the Bitches had a chance. Ha-ha." Q gave me a once-over and I knew what was coming. "So, are you gonna do something with your hair?"

"Like what?" My hair had a tendency to frizz, which bugged me to no end, but I'd never found a secret to taming it that didn't make me look like a total greaseball.

"Let's get Marlise to blow it out for you."

It would cost me all of fifteen bucks. I knew that when Q made a suggestion about my appearance, it was for my own good. I guess since I didn't have a mom to tell me I needed a new lip color or my outfit didn't match, I had Q.

We went into The Beauty Salon (which was exactly its name) and were greeted by Arlene, one of the stylists. She yelled over her shoulder. "Marlise, how long you gon' be?"

Marlise shouted back, "Ten minutes."

We sat down in styling chairs in front of the mirrors and flipped through some magazines with different hairstyles.

"Man, when are these from, 1982?" I looked down in disgust at some of the awful 'dos.

Q flipped to the front of the book. "1997. Damn, look at this one. Looks like a rat gnawed off the ends of her hair. If Marlise does that to you, I'm gonna have to kill you."

"Good. I'd do the same for you."

But in the end my hair looked fly. Sleek and straight. Like a supermodel.

For the next few hours we went our separate ways—Q to

eat dinner with her family, me to eat grilled cheese in front of the TV. I called Black Chuck and told him to be at my place at eight p.m. and don't be late. Then I turned on KTU and danced around my room, thinking of the night's possibilities.

I kept glancing at the phone, waiting for it to ring.

6 o'clock.

6:15.

6:30.

6:45.

6:52. *Brrrinnng!*

Oh please, oh please! I answered the phone. "Hello?"

"Can I speak to Julia?"

AMEN!

"That's me. Is this Eric?"

"Yeah. What up?"

"Chillin', you know. You?"

"Same. What's the plan tonight?"

"We're meeting at my place at eight. You up for it?"

"'Course I am. Where's your crib?"

I gave him directions. "It's two minutes from the bus stop. Apartment 3C."

"Got it. See you at eight."

"Bye." I hung up. Giggled. And put on some Shakira and danced.

Black Chuck arrived half an hour early, giving me a one-armed hug as he came in the door. He was in full colors, rocking blue gear from his hat to his kicks to the flag that stuck out of his back pocket. He even had a blue Band-Aid on his arm.

"Hey, Ju. Got anything to eat?"

"Some chips and stuff. Help yourself."

He went to the kitchen cupboards, pulled out some sour-cream-and-onion-chips and stuffed them between two slices of bread. Then he sat down at the kitchen table and starting eating.

"God, you *are* hungry." I put a can of Coke in front of him. "Didn't you have dinner?"

"Nah. We had a meeting."

"At your crib?"

"Yeah."

"Everything cool with Scrap?" His brother got the name from the Scooby Doo character Scrappy Doo, the little dog that liked to fight a lot. He lived up to his name.

"Scrap's a'ight." He chewed the sandwich. "Got any butter? This is dry."

"Sure." I got him some butter.

"That's better," he said after another few bites. "We got

beef with the Latin Kings and Cholos. Damn Spics been hus-tlin' in our territory."

"*Spics?*"

"C'mon, Ju. I don't mean *you*. Hell, you don't even speak Spanish."

"So? If my mom was alive, I would."

"I get the point. Anyway, these guys jumped one of our crew. Fucked up his face. So we gonna jump their head man, El Guapo. He won't even know what hit him."

"But if you jump this El Guapo, how's that gonna solve it? Won't they just strike back harder?"

"It don't matter. We gotta avenge our brother."

"Yeah, but I bet it'll make things worse."

He shrugged and chomped on his sandwich. Trying to use logic on him was tough.

"Chuck, listen. Just because Scrap has a plan doesn't mean you have to go along with it. You want to graduate, right? Why don't you take a break from this shit?"

"It don't work like that, Ju. My blood is blue."

"Whatever. I hate worrying about you, that's all."

"Worrying is my mama's job. But she too cracked up to care." He laughed.

How he could laugh at his crack-addicted mom, I didn't

know. But I guess he wasn't laughing deep down. Poor Black Chuck. His mom was in rehab *again*.

He told me a few years back that having a crack-addicted mom was worse than having no mom at all. I thought it might be true. Even though I didn't have a mom, I knew that if she were around she would be there for me and take care of me. Black Chuck's mom had let him down in every way. I used to give him quarters to buy chips for lunch, because his mom was using their welfare money to get high.

Finishing his sandwich, Black Chuck put his plate in the sink, dusted off his hands and headed for the stereo system. "Been working on some new moves. You ready?"

"Of course."

He put on some tunes and we started kickin' it: the Harlem, the robot, the slide, the World Trade Center. Then he showed me his new move that he called the 2000 Years B.C. (Before Chuck). I did it pretty well, except the low spin at the end — I didn't need to sprain my ankle.

Obie Trice came on, and Black Chuck sang along with the chorus, sung by Akon:

Anything you need, believe me, I'm gon lace you
Just don't, whatever you do, Snitch
'Cause you will get hit, pray I don't lace you, yeah

Q showed up next, looking fly in white and pink. Everything she wore matched perfectly, from nails to handbag to kicks to Victoria's Secret underwear. She had a thing about making sure her underwear matched her outerwear.

Q started dancing with us, shaking her booty like Beyoncé.

A few minutes later, I buzzed Eric in. I checked myself in the mirror before opening the door. My knees almost gave out. He was dressed totally in black, from his leather jacket to his shoes. The only flash of color was the ice around his neck—a dog tag with *Valienté* engraved in silver.

"I heard the music from the hallway, Divine. Did the party start without me?"

"No way. The party's been *waiting* for you. Come on in."

"Yo, my man!" Black Chuck pounded palms with Eric.

"You know each other?" I asked.

"The whole school knows Black Chuck," Eric said. "He lives in those halls. Man, do you ever go to class?"

"Only when security's doing hall sweeps," Black Chuck replied.

Q walked up. "Eric, right? I'm Q."

"Q?"

"Yeah. Mad ghetto, hunh?"

"Sounds more like a *Star Trek* character to me," he said, refusing to be an ass-kisser. "But it's cool."

"Glad you think so."

Eric's gaze took in the place. "Nice crib."

"Thanks. You live around here?"

"Not far. I live in Park Slope."

We all looked at each other. Park Slope was one of the richest neighborhoods in Brooklyn.

Eric laughed at us. "You guys are tripping. I live in the South Slope."

Oh, well that was still the ghetto then.

"Should we dip?" I said.

They agreed. I grabbed my knockoff Gucci handbag (fifteen down from twenty on Canal Street) and my Baby Phat jacket off the peg by the door.

We caught the elevator down and went outside. A bum sitting on the step shook his cup. Eric dropped a dollar in as we walked past.

"He's there every day," I muttered to him. "Any money you give him he'll use to buy crack."

"Maybe."

"Definitely. He lives at the Mission. Got his room and board covered. One time I said I was going to the store so I'd buy him something to eat. You know what he said? *Gimme the money instead.*"

"Oh, shit."

It was a ten-minute walk to Raoume's place on Washington Avenue. The whole way there, Eric and Black Chuck talked about *CSI*. It was cool seeing them getting along. If they started hanging out together, I'd have even more chances to see Eric outside of school.

Q and me walked a short ways behind the guys. *He is so hot!* she mouthed.

I know, I mouthed back.

She leaned close to me. "You are *so* getting freaky with him tonight. Total L.R."

Lubricated Rodeo. Where the hell she'd heard that, I didn't know. But it sounded so wrong coming out of her mouth.

She was right about one thing. I'd love to get closer to Eric tonight. But was he even interested?

Why shouldn't he be? I thought. *I'm cute, aren't I?*

But I'd rather be beautiful. Stunningly beautiful with raven-black hair, ice-blue eyes, a slim, upturned nose and dimples. Maybe three inches taller.

But instead of being beautiful, I was cute. Everyone said I was. Sweet. Some even said I looked innocent.

And I knew why. It was because I had a baby face. A nice heart-shaped face and a pretty smile (minus crooked eyetooth.) Damn that baby face. Guys didn't want cute. They wanted sexy. They wanted *hot*.

Well, I knew what I wanted.

To kiss someone.

Not just anyone.

Eric.

Tonight.

THE PARTY

Raoume's crib was already jumping when we got there. His friend, Salvatori, was spinning the sounds. A huge black guy patted us down at the door. He stopped Black Chuck. "Gimme the flag."

Black Chuck reluctantly gave it to him.

Walking into the living room was like stepping into a dance club. Strobe lights flashed, putting everything in slow motion. Most people were dancing, except for a couple of kids on the couch. The smell of weed hung in the air, mixed with heavy perfume.

Q looked at us. "We gonna dance?"

"Later," Black Chuck said. "I'm thirsting for some Hennessy. Bet my bro Eric is too."

"You got it."

We went down the hall toward the bedrooms, squeezing through a bunch of people. The bar was in Raoume's bedroom. A table was set up with bottles and a hoochie-type behind it. We went up to the bar and ordered an Appletini for me, an Incredible Hulk for Q, Bacardi Silver for Eric, and straight Hennessy for Black Chuck. Eric thrust out a twenty before anybody could argue.

We left the bedroom with our drinks and headed into another, bigger bedroom crowded with people. Black Chuck pounded palms all the way there.

The RLB girls were there, no surprise. They weren't rocking their colors—smart, since Flatbush was mostly a Crip hood. Marie separated from them to give Q and me hugs. "What's good, honeys? See you got some manpower behind ya. That Eric is hot! You better keep an eye on him because my Bitches are interested."

"You can tell them Eric is taken," Q said.

"I will. But that won't stop them from trying."

I had a sinking feeling in my stomach. Whatever. If Eric was stupid enough to fall into their trap, then I didn't want him anyway.

After we finished our drinks, me and Q tried to get the

guys to come dance with us, but they were too busy talking to Chuck's friends. I told myself it was okay; I couldn't blame Eric for wanting to meet people.

We blazed on the dance floor, pulling some hot moves out of our arsenal of weapons: the chickenhead, the dip, and, of course, Q's booty shake. With the tunes spinning around us and the martini in my bloodstream, I was feeling fast, sexy, alive.

We'd been dancing for at least an hour when I felt someone bump my ass. Eric slid up behind me and grabbed my hips. He wanted to grind! I glanced back at him, at his wicked smile, and went with it.

Meanwhile Q was dubbin' in front of Black Chuck. They looked good together. But Q was a square girl, and Chuck spent too much time on the wrong side of right. It would never work.

Eric moved so well, fluid and sensual, that I felt myself getting heated up. Eventually, we collapsed on the sofa.

"You know how to move, Divine."

"I was thinking the same about you. Is this what the parties in Detroit are like?"

"Yeah." His eyes were far off for a minute.

"You miss your friends?"

"Sometimes. But I'm not missing anyone right now." God,

he had soulful dark eyes. "You're cute, Julia. You know that?"

Cute! He means it in a good way, I told myself. *Just go with it.*

"I'll take your word for it."

"Yo, Eric!" It was Black Chuck, out of breath from dancing. "My boy's here. Come on."

Eric looked at me. "I'll be back in a few."

"Okay."

Q replaced him on the couch. "Man, Chuck knows how to dance."

"Yeah."

"Too bad he doesn't have much upstairs."

"Q! That's mean."

"I know, I know. I love Chuck too. But it's true, don't you think? He only passed one class last year and that was basketball. And he was just bragging to me that he's tried a hundred different types of weed. Sorry to say, but that boy needs a hobby."

"You're right about that."

"That's what they're doing right now, you know—smoking up in the bedroom."

"Oh." I felt a stab of disappointment. Not that a little weed was a big deal, but I'd been hoping Eric wouldn't bother with those things. Well, hopefully he wasn't a devotee like Black Chuck.

"What'd you expect, Julia? He's from Detroit. Weed's probably nothing for him. I bet he's done heavier shit than that. Should we check up on him?"

"Nah. That's his business, not mine."

"High school guys are so wack," Q said. "I'm gonna get myself a college guy."

Soon after, we hit the dance floor again. It became mad obvious that Eric had forgotten his promise to come back *in a few*. I couldn't help feeling hurt and a little pissed off.

By midnight, I'd had enough of the party. I told Q that I was going home.

"Mom's picking me up at twelve thirty," she said. "Wait a bit and she'll drive you."

"Thanks, but I'll be fine." I hugged her. "I'll call you tomorrow."

I said "bye" to a couple of people on my way out, but I wasn't going to stop in the bedroom to tell the guys I was leaving.

A ten-minute walk seemed a lot longer when it's dark and you're alone. So I tightened the laces of my shoes and did what I usually did when it wasn't safe: I ran.

I jogged across the parking lot in front of Raoumc's building. The streets weren't totally deserted; I saw a few guys my age hanging out in the doorway of an all-night deli. I ran to the corner of Church Avenue, stopping to catch my breath. And then I heard it.

My name.

I swung around to find Eric running up to me. He stopped in front of me, much less winded than I was. "What are you running for?"

"To be safer, I guess."

"Why didn't you tell me you were leaving?"

I shrugged. "I didn't want to interrupt."

"You should've. It's stupid walking home by yourself."

"I wasn't *walking*. Anyway, I'm a black belt."

He crossed his arms. "Yeah, sure."

"Fine, I'm lying. You should go back to the party." I sniffed. "Chocolate weed, hunh?"

He lifted a brow. "Something wrong with that?"

"No. I'm just not into that."

"Me neither, most of the time. Look, you probably think I ditched you, but I really didn't. I got caught up in things. My bad." He slung an arm around me. "Why don't I walk you the rest of the way home?"

"I won't stop you."

It felt surreal, having his arm around me, his warm body

brushing up against mine as we walked. He'd actually come after me. That *must* mean something.

"That Black Chuck is hilarious," he said. "No offense, but it's kinda weird thinking you two are friends. You're totally different."

"Yeah, but we go way back. We're like family, maybe because our families aren't the best. I mean, my dad is great, but I don't see him that much. And Black Chuck's mom isn't around."

"What about his brother, Scrap? He talks about him like he's a god."

"Scrap is head of the Flatbush Junction Crips."

"I heard."

"FJC's always got drama going on. Chuck's more concerned with the latest beef than anything else in his life — like school. Sometimes I worry Chuck's gonna get hurt."

"I think our man BC can take care of himself."

"I hope so. I'm always telling him to be careful, but he never listens. I wish he'd get out of the gang."

"You gotta respect his choices, Julia. He knows what he's doing."

"Who are you, Oprah?"

"With her cash flow, I *wish*."

I was actually disappointed when we reached the lobby of

my building, and I had to move away from him to press the button for the elevator. The doors opened right away.

"Thanks for walking me."

"Wait a second, Julia."

He jammed the elevator door with his foot, touched my cheek softly, and pressed his lips against mine. I was so stunned that it took me a couple of seconds to respond. I parted my lips to kiss him back. He smiled against my lips, made a *mmm* sound and kissed me more deeply.

My mind reeled. I was kissing Eric! No, Eric was kissing *me*! And it was awesome. This guy knew how to kiss—slow and sensual, without too much saliva or tongue. His lips were driving me crazy, making my eyeballs roll back behind my lids, making my body burn for him.

Beep, beep.

Damn it! The elevator made that annoying sound when you held it longer than ten seconds.

Eric pulled back. "Wow."

"Wow," I echoed.

"I just had to . . . Hope it's okay, Divine."

"It's more than okay."

He smiled crookedly. I stepped back into the elevator, the doors closing on his beautiful face.

[YBER SPACE

EricAllStar2007: thought i might find u here divine

PoeticJustiss: no way—eric!?! howd u find out my IM?

EricAllStar2007: black chuck. did u have fun friday night?

PoeticJustiss: raoumes parties r always off da hook

EricAllStar2007: i meant somethin else ;-)

PoeticJustiss: OMG! well u saw me smiling didnt u?

that satisfy ur ego?

EricAllStar2007: fo sho!

PoeticJustiss: so what u mean by that kiss anyway?

EricAllStar2007: lol u know damn well what it means.

means I wanna come over to ur crib RIGHT

NOW and do it again! and again and again . . .

PoeticJustiss: r u tryin to have cyber sex with me?

67

EricAllStar2007:   not cyber

PoeticJustiss: ERIC!

EricAllStar2007:   im playin. when can i c u?

PoeticJustiss: um . . . sometime this week i guess

EricAllStar2007:   why u hesitate?

PoeticJustiss: cyber-stutter???

EricAllStar2007:   u r crazy. so wat u wanna do and when?

PoeticJustiss: hmmm . . . wednesday we get outta
                    school early for p/t conferences. lets
                    hang after that

EricAllStar2007:   wednesday thats in 3 days! ok i will wait

PoeticJustiss: well i CANT WAIT to c u

EricAllStar2007:   damn u sweet divine

{LOUD NINE

"Julia!"

I lifted my head from the desk to find Mr. Finklestein glaring at me.

"Awake now?"

I blinked, trying to clear the cobwebs from my head. "Yeah. Sorry."

He gave me the *I expected better from you* shake of the head. "As I was saying . . ."

It was the second time this week I'd been caught dozing in his class, and I was a little disappointed in myself. I'd never wanted to be one of those girls who let school suffer because of a guy.

But Eric wasn't just any guy. He was *Eric*.

It all started with the phenomenal kiss.

Since then, we'd IM'ed and talked on the phone every night. His phone voice was ultra-sexy. So many things about him surprised and impressed me. Like he was a total fan of *CSI* and *Law and Order*. Like he was on the All-Star baseball *and* basketball teams last year. Like he was an extra in a few indie music videos. Like when he was tired he let Spanish words slip.

The one thing he didn't want to say was why he came to Brooklyn in the first place, but I knew I'd get it out of him. Maybe today after school when we had our first date.

Suddenly everybody got up and started moving their desks. I guess we'd been assigned some group work. I joined a group and looked at the board to figure out our instructions.

"Are you doing it with Eric yet?" asked Kareen, well known for her big mouth.

I groaned. "If it happens, you'll be the first to know."

"I bet he'd be mad good," Kareen said.

"He's brolic, all right," Jessica put in. "But I thought you was with Black Chuck."

"Black Chuck and I were always just friends." I raised my hand and asked Mr. Finklestein if he was collecting the classwork assignment. He said he was, so I tried to curb the convo so that we could get some work done.

I figured this would be an easy day because of the early dismissal. I couldn't wait to see Eric. We were going to catch a movie then get some eats at TGI Friday's.

At 12:35 p.m., we met at the gates in front of the school, just as floods of kids were coming out. I was standing with Marie and Q, trying not to get trampled.

Eric touched the small of my back. It gave me a little shiver. "We good to go?"

"Yeah." I paused as two Crip girls, Sarah and Nessa, walked by, their eyes hating on Marie.

I heard Nessa say, "Nice pants, Marie."

Marie got her back up. I, for one, liked her jeans with the hand painted over the left butt cheek, even if they weren't my style.

Too bad Marie couldn't let the comment go.

She put an arm out in front of Nessa. "You like 'em, huh?"

"Yeah, I do." Nessa sucked on her blue lollipop. "The hand on your ass is mad *phat*."

None of us missed the double meaning.

"You were looking at my ass? 'Cause you wouldn't have seen the hand if you weren't looking at my ass." Marie smacked her butt. "You want a piece?"

"Sorry, but I don't go that way," Nessa said. "Though you got enough ass there to feed a Third World country."

"A *what?*" Marie pushed her. Nessa pushed back. Then they were grabbing, tearing, grunting.

That's how the riot started. Within two seconds, everybody knew there was a fight and rushed in. They closed in before Eric, Q, or me had a chance to pull the girls apart.

Picture it: thousands of students all being let out at the same time, a fight waiting for them. Everybody full of energy because we got out early. "Fight, fight," charging through the air.

More fights broke out, like little wildfires, throughout the crowd. Gang members. Honors students. It didn't matter anymore. A wave of people spilled into the streets, stopping the traffic on Avenue X. Some of them surrounded cars, banging on the trunks and hoods, cursing at the drivers, who got out and cursed back.

Q and I stood there, watching it all from the school lawn. Eric headed for a confrontation between a skinny Puerto Rican kid and a beefy white driver. I watched, my heart in my throat, as Eric stepped between them, taking the man by the shoulders, somehow managing to talk him out of beating the kid to a pulp with his antitheft device. The kid ran away, and Eric coaxed the guy back into his car.

Sirens filled the air as the NYPD pulled up on all sides. It looked like a squirt of soap dropped into a pool of grease as kids ran off in all directions.

Marie emerged from the crowd, her hair wild.

"You okay?" I asked.

She nodded and cracked her gum. "Wasn't no more room to fight." She looked disappointed. "Y'all like my jeans, don't ya?"

FIRST DATE

The Rock was nothing compared to Eric. It wasn't the Rock's hard body leaning into mine in spite of the armrest. It wasn't the Rock's hand on my thigh during *the entire movie*. He was just on the screen in some mindless action flick. I paid him no attention.

TGI Friday's was steps away from the movie theater on Knapp Street. The place was pretty empty, so we had our choice of tables. We chose a booth, of course.

Eric slid in across from me, putting his forearms on the table. "What did you think?"

"Of what?"

"The movie!"

"Oh. It was all right."

"C'mon, I know you *ain't* one of those girls who don't have opinions."

"Okay, how about it sucked?"

"You're right, it did. Next time you choose."

"Next time I will."

The waitress came over and handed us menus. "Something to drink to start off?"

"I'll have a virgin strawberry daiquiri." I turned to Eric. "They have the best daiquiris here."

"I'll have a Corona."

"Do you have ID?" the waitress asked.

"Sure." He pulled ID out of his wallet.

She looked at it and gave it back to him. "I'll be right back with your drinks."

She walked off. He slid the ID over to me. It was a Michigan driver's license with his picture on it. His real name too. And a birth date making him twenty-one years old.

"How'd you get this?"

"I got connections in DT. Good, eh? Cost me enough."

"How much?"

"Two hundred."

"Holy shit!"

"It's worth it. Gives me the freedom to go wherever I want. Can't put a price tag on that."

I examined it closely. "It's flawless. You can see it was done by a pro."

"I know. Nobody gives me a hard time with that. Doesn't hurt that most of my friends in Detroit are older anyway."

I looked up at him, my eyes narrowing. "How old are you?"

"Eighteen. Got held back in eighth grade. So I'm past wanting to get the hell out of high school."

"I hear that. What about after you graduate?"

"I'll sponge off my parents my whole life, being from a rich family and all."

"Spare me."

"Okay, my real answer is, I'm gonna be a chef. It'll take years to make a name for myself in the industry, but once I do, I'll get some investors and open my own restaurant. Most of the top chefs own or at least partly own their restaurants. That's how you make the real money and how you get creative control."

Wow. He'd really thought this through.

I could see it now: *Valienté*, the hottest restaurant in

Manhattan, with a waiting list several weeks long and every-one dying to catch a glimpse of the hot chef.

Oops, he was still talking. ". . . fusion, Caribbean, Japa-nese. I want to get good at everything before I specialize."

"You can practice on me anytime."

He answered with a grin, and I blushed. I hadn't meant it *that* way, but I wasn't sorry he took it that way either.

The waitress came back with the drinks. I took a long sip of mine. It was so good, it didn't need alcohol.

"Try some," I offered.

"Sure." He pulled the straw toward him and sipped. I watched, mesmerized, as the strong muscles in his throat swallowed. He was using my straw, I thought dreamily. I wouldn't share my straw with just anyone. It was sharing DNA after all.

Eric made a face. "That's way too sweet. Tastes like Kool-Aid."

"Sweet isn't a bad thing."

"Try my beer." He slid it in front of me.

I took a tentative sip from the bottle. "It's not bad, for beer."

"I love it. In Mexico, they leave the worm in it. You hun-gry?" He looked at the menu.

"I think I'll have mozzarella sticks."

"I'll have the nachos grande. We can share."

He flagged down the waitress and ordered, then said, "What were we talking about? Oh yeah. You got a plan after graduation?"

"Lately I've been thinking about psychology."

"I could see that. I'd drop some cash to lie on a couch and tell you my problems."

I raised an eyebrow. "I'm here right now. You can tell me for free. You never told me what kind of trouble you got into in Detroit."

"*Damn*, you don't let up, do you? Okay, then. I'm here because I got into a few fights and got too many suspensions."

"You don't seem really aggressive or anything."

"I mind my business. But when I see people going after my friends, I don't walk away."

I frowned. "Who can blame you for sticking up for your friends?"

"Everybody can. At my school, it didn't matter who started the fight—if you're involved, you get suspended. After three suspensions, they put me on academic probation. Mom had enough."

"That's horrid."

"Yeah. Anyway, I was glad to come to Brooklyn. I couldn't stand her being on my case."

"How are things with your dad?"

"They're cool. He knows I'm an adult, lets me do my thing. But it's only temporary, living with my dad. As soon as I get the money, I'm moving out. You get along with your dad?"

"Yeah. He's like yours I guess—lets me do whatever I want. He trusts me."

"My mom never trusted me. She thought I was always looking for trouble."

"She'll realize her mistake eventually."

"I hope so." He paused, then a smile touched his lips. "You know, if somebody'd told me I'd meet a girl as smart and cute as you in Brooklyn, I wouldn't have believed it."

"I never expected a guy from Detroit would be so sweet."

"A lot of things about me might surprise you, Divine."

I stirred my daiquiri, not sure what that meant, but loving the mystery.

EricAllStar2007:   i had a great time today
PoeticJustiss: not better than i did
EricAllStar2007:   when can i see u again? friday night?

PoeticJustiss: i cant its a girls night at melishas

EricAllStar2007:   girls night . . . thats wat girls do when they dont have boyfriends right? u dont have to go do u?

PoeticJustiss: im not gonna ditch my friends

EricAllStar2007:   props 2 u. saturday night then?

PoeticJustiss: i think i can swing that. better check my schedule :)

EricAllStar2007:   how about i come over n make u dinner?

PoeticJustiss: that would be great!!

EricAllStar2007:   ur dad wont be home will he?

PoeticJustiss: he usually works saturdays and spends the night at his gf's. wat u dont wanna chill wit my dad?

EricAllStar2007:   at some point sure but right now i want u all 2 myself

PoeticJustiss: wat r u getting at?

EricAllStar2007:   just wat it sounds like. would be cool to be alone . . . don't u think?

PoeticJustiss: yeah but . . .

EricAllStar2007:   im no dog . . . well ok every guy is . . . but u dont have to worry im not gonna pressure u

to do anything u dont wanna do. thats not
just talk its the truth.

PoeticJustiss: thanx eric. means a lot. anyway u wouldnt
have much luck if u tried

EricAllStar2007:   lol i got u divine

ꟼIRLZ NIGHT

"Crap, I left the chips at home." I buzzed Melisha's crib.

"I brought three bags of Doritos," Q said. "They'll be from both of us."

"Thanks."

Melisha buzzed us in. We caught the elevator as the door was closing. A couple of baggy-pants homies caught a glimpse of Q's chest and looked at each other. I shrugged my shoulders as if to say, *Yeah, I know my friend's a hottie*. They smiled gold-toothed smiles as if to say, *You ain't bad yourself*.

I wondered how Eric would feel if he saw me smiling at these guys. He didn't seem like the jealous type. But I wouldn't mind if he was a *little* bit jealous.

Melisha's place smelled of spicy Caribbean cooking — today I guessed jerk chicken. Shared by Melisha and her mom, the crib was small but made cozy by brightly colored throws and cushions.

The girls' night agenda was always the same:

Gossip.

Junk food.

Guy talk (also falls under gossip category).

TV watching.

And gross talk (sentences starting with: *The most disgusting thing I ever . . .*)

When we came in, the girls were watching Chapelle's Show on DVD. Q squeezed in between Marie and Vicky on the couch, and I sat cross-legged on the carpet.

After laughing so hard we almost peed, the *guy talk* started.

Vicky started us off. "C'mon now, who's the hottest guy in school?"

"Sean Avila," Marie said. "It ain't even a question."

"Oh, right." Vicky giggled.

There were nods all around. A junior at our school, Sean Avila was the kind of hot that made you look three times. You could dream about him but you could never have him. And it's probably better you didn't have him, because he was a big-time drug dealer.

"I got a new Sean story!" Melisha said.

Marie rolled her eyes. "We heard it a thousand times already. It ain't even a story."

I perked up. "I didn't hear it."

Melisha licked her glossy lips. "So it was Tuesday afternoon and I was late for class. And who do I run into the basement hallway?"

"Mr. Finklestein?" I teased.

"Don't be a wiseass. Sean, of course. Just strolling along like it's a nice sunny day instead of a dark stinking basement. And I'm not sure if I should look at him or not, because you know, we don't really talk or anything. So I just give him a little smile, and then he says, '*Hey shorty.*'"

I waited for the next part of the story until I realized there wasn't one.

"Did you hear that? He called me 'shorty'!"

I smiled. "That's cool."

"It's because he don't know your name," Marie said. "Went to school with you for half your life and he don't know your name. And now he'll never know because . . ." She paused way longer than she had to. "He got kicked out!"

We gasped.

"It's true," Marie said. "Schmidt's been trying to get him out for a long time. He finally got his way."

We looked at one another, speechless.

Breaking our moment of silence, Melisha said, "It's so unfair!" By unfair, I figured she meant the fact that she might never see him again—not the fact that he'd been kicked out.

"Okay, let's get back to business," Vicky said. "Who is the hottest guy at school now that Sean got kicked out?"

"I think Ben Rice's the hottest senior," Q said, "but not according to Julia."

I smiled.

"Eric's too skinny for me." Marie grabbed a handful of chips. "I bet he don't even have an ass."

I almost spilled my soda. "He's not skinny at all. And he does have an ass. You should look for yourself!"

The girls burst out laughing.

Okay, I'd overreacted.

"I'm playing!" Marie said. "But I'll have a look next time I see him."

"Go on and look," I said, "as long as you don't touch."

"I'd never touch your man. Anyway, Black Chuck's gotta be one of the hottest guys in school."

"If you're feenin' for him, you should go for him," Vicky said.

Marie snorted. "Yeah, right. A Blood Bitch with a Crip nigga? I'd get the shit kicked outta me. And I'd deserve it too."

Their attention was grabbed by an episode of *Cribs* in which Pharrell gave the cameras a tour of his Malibu beach house. As I sat back and munched on chips, I fantasized about living in such a beautiful house. I could afford it because I was an award-winning poet. Maybe I'd be married to world-famous chef and restaurateur, Eric Valienté . . .

Melisha nudged me with her elbow. "Well?"

"Hunh?"

"Who is the *last* person you'd ever sleep with at South Bay?"

Apparently the *gross talk* had started. "Mr. McLennan," I said. "His belly's so huge I want to prick it with a pin and see if it pops."

They enjoyed that.

"I'd say that cafeteria monitor." Q twisted her mouth. "What's his name? The one with the horrible teeth?"

"*Ughhh!*" came from everyone.

"I wouldn't let that man touch me for a million dollars," Marie said.

"I'd pay *him* a million dollars to stop him from touching me." Vicky shuddered.

We'd had this conversation, or some variation of it, about a million times already. Most of the time I wouldn't care, but I'd passed up a night with Eric for this.

I wondered what he was doing right now.

About twelve thirty, Q finally called her mom to pick us up. A good thing since I could have conked out any second on the fuzzy carpet.

Q's Mom didn't like her riding the train or bus too late at night, so she usually came to get us. My dad didn't like it either, so he gave me a cell phone. Unless the cell phone had a switchblade function I hadn't discovered, I doubted it would be much help against an attacker. But I was glad to have the phone, and bought myself some pepper spray just in case I had an attacker who wouldn't wait for me to dial 911.

As we waited for her mom to buzz, I texted Eric.

ON MY WAY HOME. MISS U. SLEEP TITE.

Q didn't need to ask who I was texting. She just smiled a knowing smile.

When her mom showed up, we hopped in. I liked Louise

Stairs. She was a hard-ass, but she could giggle like a little girl if you caught her in the right mood.

My phone vibrated against my hip. A text message from Eric!

MISS U MORE. MEET ME NOW UNION SQ/16 ST OUTSIDE COF-FEE SHOP PLEEZ BOO!

Meet him *now*?

It was ridiculous. A no-brainer. It was way too late. I was already on my way home.

My fingers were poised to text him back.

He *did* call me *boo*.

Forget it. I wasn't so hungry for an Eric fix that I needed to see him right now. Who was I kidding?

I wrote: U CRAZY OK IM COMIN W8T 4 ME. I fired off the message.

"Could you drop me off at the F train, please?" I asked Ms. Stairs.

"Why?" she and Q asked at the same time.

"I'm meeting Eric in the city."

"You're insane," Q said.

"It's almost one o'clock," her mom added.

"Yeah, but I already said I would."

"Text him back and tell him you changed your mind," Q said.

"Why would I do that?"

"Because you'll be taking the train home in the middle of the night and it's dangerous."

"I'll take a taxi."

"You know how much that'll cost?"

"I got it covered."

"Have you heard of those cabbies who drive girls to the wrong place and rape them?"

"Q." We were getting close to the station. "You can drop me off just up here."

For a second I thought Ms. Stairs might say no, but she stopped the car. "Just be careful, Julia."

"I will. Thanks. 'Night!"

I shut the door. Swiping my MetroCard, I went to the underground platform to wait for the train. It was cool that Q cared so much, but sometimes she overdid it. She was the one who had to follow the strict rules, not me.

I tapped my foot waiting for the train to come. I wasn't tired anymore. The thought of seeing Eric was like a shot of caffeine to my bloodstream.

SPOKEN WORD

I saw him first, standing with his hands in his pockets at the top of the stairs.

He saw me second, flashed me a smile.

When I got to the top of the steps, he wrapped his arms around me. "I been dying to see you, Divine. I couldn't wait till tomorrow night."

"Actually tomorrow night is tonight."

"True that." He grabbed my hand. "Where do you wanna go?"

"Anywhere."

"Anywhere *you* can get in." He laughed. "I know a place."

And he did—a softly lit lounge with comfy couches and

earthy tones, its walls spattered with local artwork. Call it a mix of bar and café, with a chill clientele and music low enough you didn't have to shout. There were no doormen to ask for ID, but after we found seats Eric went up to the bar by himself, just in case they felt like carding.

I told him to surprise me, and he brought back glasses of red wine.

"Vino Italiano para Miss DiVino."

"Thanks. I love this place. How'd you find out about it?"

"Dad used to take me here when I was visiting. In the daytime it's more like a café. They've got great hot chocolate."

I sipped the wine. It was damn good, not that I knew anything about wine. I couldn't believe I was at a place like this, all arty and sophisticated. I should've probably felt weird with these elegant Manhattan twenty-somethings around, but with Eric by my side, I held my own.

I noticed girls eyeing him since the moment we got here. But then they figured it out: *Eric's with me*.

"So what were you doing tonight?" I asked.

"Nothing much. Played some pool with Black Chuck and his homies, then got something to eat. How was your girls' night thing?"

"Same old. I was distracted, I guess."

An eyebrow lifted. "Oh yeah? Why?"

I shrugged, trying to hold back a smile.

"Distracted in the same way I been distracted?"

"Maybe."

Our eyes fused, and we both felt it. And it wasn't a maybe.

My eyes drifted over the low-lit room, the stylish people talking, the paintings on the walls. I checked out a painting near my head that looked like blood splatters against a white background. Price tag: three hundred and fifty dollars.

"You gotta be kidding me," Eric said, following my eyes. "I could do that blindfolded."

"For sure." I angled my head. "I'm sure the artist would say it's got some deep meaning. All I see are blood splatters."

"Do you? I thought it looked like juice that dripped on a white floor."

"Are you saying I've got a sick mind? Look how red it is."

He grinned. "You watch too many movies. Blood ain't that red most of the time. It's dark and thick like black cherry juice."

"I guess I won't ask how you know."

"Yeah, no point." He looked back at the painting. "So you write, huh? Poetry? How's that going?"

"Good." I almost mentioned the Writers' Club contest, but decided not to. It would be embarrassing if I wasn't one of the winners. "I like to play with words, put things in different ways."

"Yeah, I know what you mean. I wrote some stuff too. I liked to write stories in verse. My English teacher thought I should enter contests." He shrugged.

"Well, did you?"

"Nah. She wanted to mess with my stuff, so why bother?"

"I don't see anything wrong with letting somebody change a few small things. All writers and poets have people who do that."

"That's not the type of thing I mean. She said she wanted to make it better, but she really wanted to change the whole meaning of it."

"How did she want to change it?" I asked.

"Well, I wrote this story called 'Peep,' about a guy walking the streets one day and everything he peeped."

"That's an amazing idea! What did he see?"

"He saw an old lady pushing her walker. Kids skipping

rope. People waiting for the bus. Life, you know? So my teacher said I gotta add something more dramatic. She said I must've seen something dramatic on the streets I could write about, like a carjacking or a drive-by. *That* would really get the judges' attention."

"But you didn't want to change it."

"Nah, I wouldn't change it. I told her I don't write tragedy. I don't see why somebody has to die or get hurt for it to be good. Sometimes it's good if nothing much happens. If it's just a normal no-drama day. But she didn't get it."

He watched me over the rim of his glass, and I could tell he was hoping that I got it.

"I'm glad you didn't change it, Eric."

"If I had, I might be a grand richer. But I'm glad I didn't too."

Eric sipped his wine, smiled. Eric was turning out to be so much more than I expected.

I woke up with the scent of him on my skin. Must've been from all that nuzzling in the cab.

The clock read 1:44 p.m. That was no surprise, since I got in sometime past 5 a.m.

I rolled over, hugging the covers, wishing they were him.

Eric, Eric, Eric. I closed my eyes to relive last night. The memory was like a dream, vivid, trancelike. I'd started out sitting across from him; by the end of the night, I'd been curled in his lap. I could still feel his breath on my cheek and his lips against my neck.

He was so different than any other guy. He could talk about something just to explore it, instead of always turning things around to make them about him. It wasn't what I would've expected from a bad boy from Detroit.

Maybe I'd got the bad boy part wrong.

He didn't talk much about his life in Detroit, but when he did, he talked with a lightness that his eyes didn't carry off. Maybe that darkness was just a part of who he was. Or maybe it came from the type of experiences that made you know what blood really looks like. I didn't know. All I knew was that I wasn't going to push him to tell me more than he wanted to. He'd come to Brooklyn to start over, clean slate, and that meant letting go of the past.

I sighed, wondering if I should have let Eric stay over. Dad had spent the night at Gina's, of course, and though he usually came home to shower and change before his Saturday shift, it wouldn't have been hard to have Eric over without him ever knowing about it.

But then, if Eric had stayed over, he might've kept kissing me that way he does, and he might've kept staring at me with that hunger that made me ache.

If he'd stayed over, there wouldn't have been any sleep at all.

FEVER

I dangled out the door as Eric came up the hallway. In faded jeans and a leather jacket, he was amazing.

He cupped my waist and backed me into the apartment, giving me a long, mind-spinning kiss. It lit me up inside, reminding me that last night had been real.

"How are you feeling today?" he asked.

"Great. Why wouldn't I be?"

He laughed. "You were a little tipsy last night. I couldn't believe it. You only had two glasses of wine." He squeezed my waist. "Lightweight."

"I slept it off."

"I see that." He leaned forward, burying his face in my hair. "God, you smell good, Divine."

The nickname sent tingles down my spine. Divine. Which, according to the dictionary, meant, *Godly, or with heavenly qualities*.

"Ready to get your eat on?" he asked.

"Sure am."

"Good. I'm making sancocho, my favorite Dominican dish." He spun me out of his arms and started unloading his knapsack: fresh cilantro, plantains, onion, potatoes, meats . . . I picked up one of the packages. "We're having *goat?*"

He grinned. "You're gonna love it. It's one of the three meats I'm using: chicken, goat, and smoked ham. Some people use more." He pulled five little spice jars out of his knapsack. "I forgot to ask if you had spices, so I brought my own. Where are the pots?"

I got out several pots and watched him take control of the kitchen. I could tell he'd cooked this dish before because he seemed to know exactly what to do without the help of a recipe.

"Should I peel some potatoes?" I asked.

"Sure."

As I peeled, I kept glancing at him. I just knew that his dream of being a chef was going to be reality one day. It was refreshing as hell to find a guy who knew where he was going in life, unlike Joe, who hadn't had a clue, or Black Chuck, who'd be lucky to graduate high school.

And I couldn't believe that Eric, this guy who was driven, this guy who had goals, this guy who was *hot*, was actually cooking me dinner. When was the last time anyone had done that? Maybe my grandma last Christmas. Definitely not my dad.

An hour later, we sat down to eat. I closed my eyes as the flavors melted on my tongue. "Wow."

"Yeah?"

"Yeah." I gulped another mouthful before saying, "I hope you won't forget me when I'm trying to make a reservation at your restaurant some day."

"Forget you? You're gonna co-own it with me."

I wished!

I refilled my bowl twice before I could admit that I was full. Neither of us had room for dessert, which was good, since all I had was cheap drugstore cookies.

Piling the dishes in the sink and promising myself I'd do them in the morning, I went to the couch. Eric was looking at the pictures on the mantle.

"This has to be your mom." He picked up a framed picture of her smiling face.

"Think I look like her?"

"Yeah, I do."

"But she's got . . . a sparkling something, you know? Something about her that's just beautiful."

He looked at me, suddenly serious. "You got that, too, Julia."

"No, I don't. Not the way she had it. But one day . . . one day maybe I will."

"Did your dad take this picture?" he asked.

"Yeah. You can tell she was looking at the man she loved when the picture was taken. Doesn't she look so happy?"

"She does." He put the picture down carefully. "Your dad must've been devastated to lose her."

"They say we're lucky if we ever find the one person who's perfect for us. My parents found each other."

Eric came over to the couch and sat beside me. "You always surprise me, Divine."

"How?"

Turning to me, he slid a hand into my hair. "You just do." He kissed me.

Sliding my arms around his neck, I opened my mouth against his. Need for him poured through me. I wanted his body, his heart, his soul to be mine.

He pulled back slightly, his dark lashes shielding his eyes like tinted windows. I could feel his heat and his heartbeat against me, and I knew he was trying to keep himself in check.

He kissed me again, taking my breath away. It thrilled me and scared me at the same time.

"Eric, did you mean what you said in the IM?"

"About what?"

"That whatever I choose to do is cool . . . I mean, in terms of sex."

"Of course I meant it."

"I just wanted to make sure."

"Come here." He hugged me, and I relaxed against his chest, feeling my tension ebb. It was all good, Eric and me. Just like I'd hoped.

I felt his lips travel down the side of my neck, gently nipping and kissing. Then we heard a key turn in the door.

We sprang apart like we'd been splashed with cold water. I smoothed my hair just as my dad walked in. Seeing us on the couch, he scowled.

"Uh, Dad, this is Eric. He's a new friend of mine."

"Pleased to meet you, Mr. DiVino." I was impressed at how unfazed Eric was. He couldn't have been more casual if we'd been sitting there talking baseball. He got up, offering his hand.

Dad gave Eric a once-over (clean-cut, check, no visible piercings or tattoos, check), shook his hand and smiled. I knew he'd like him.

"Eric's been looking forward to meeting you, Dad."

Dad turned to Eric. "Is that right?"

"Yes, sir. I heard you work for the MTA. I'm taking urban planning as an elective. I have a few questions for you." Damn, he was smooth.

"Oh yeah?" Dad went to the fridge. "Want a beer, Eric? Then I'll tell you about my job."

I leaned back. *Yeah, they're going to get along just fine.*

PoeticJustiss:	my dad loves u
EricAllStar2007:	yea right
PoeticJustiss:	seriously he said ur a very mature young man n he isnt easily impressed
EricAllStar2007:	good i got him fooled lol
PoeticJustiss:	when can i meet ur dad?
EricAllStar2007:	why bother?
PoeticJustiss:	i dunno i figured were seein each other n all
EricAllStar2007:	i dont tell my dad anything thats going on in

my life. he doesnt need to know i have a girlfriend. i do don't i?

PoeticJustiss: yea u sure do. its up to u, i don't see wat the big deal is.

EricAllStar2007: me neither, its not like we gettin married or anythin

PoeticJustiss: ud never be *that* lucky

EricAllStar2007: lol dont be too sure about that. anyway my dad isnt exactly citizen of the year. hes not smart like ur dad. i dont see u getting along, ud call him a sexist pig

PoeticJustiss: i wouldnt to his face lol

EricAllStar2007: yea but u get the pic. eventually ull meet him just not now

PoeticJustiss: i understand

EricAllStar2007: i knew u would. i CANT WAIT to c u again divine

PoeticJustiss: me too. night Eric

EricAllStar2007: back atcha

I couldn't go to bed yet. I felt a poem in me. I'd call it, simply, "He."

He is dark, mysterious.
A Stranger to Brooklyn
But familiar
With its ways.
Unafraid of the dark side,
Of the Hood,
Of Himself.
A Shady Past
A Brighter Future
With Divine
Beside Him.

JUMPED IN

Eric didn't show up at his first class the next morning.

No big deal. He liked to sleep in.

When he didn't appear for the second or third, I knew something was up.

I called his cell.

"Hey Divine." I heard traffic in the background.

"Where are you?"

"On my way to school. I decided to take the morning off. Meet me at the bleachers at twelve fifteen?"

"I'll be there."

I showed up at the bleachers ten minutes early. Turned out he was ten minutes late. Eventually I saw him come around the corner onto Batchelder Avenue. He was walking slower than usual. As he got closer, panic shot through me.

"What happened to your face?" I demanded. "Who did this to you?"

When he tried to smile, I noticed that one of his front teeth was chipped. Oh, no! Who the hell messed with my boyfriend's perfect smile?

"It looks worse than it is, Divine. I was just messing around."

"Messing around? You've got a black eye. And your face is cut!" The thought of somebody hurting Eric made me sick inside. I hugged him.

He winced and stepped back. "Bruised ribs."

"Did you see a doctor?"

"It's not that serious."

"How do you know your ribs are bruised and not broken?"

"I can tell. Even if they were, there's nothing they can do about broken ribs."

"So, what happened?"

"Well, I kinda did it to myself."

"You're not making sense, Eric."

"I was with my buddies in the FJC and . . ."

I frowned. "Since when do you hang out with them?"

"Since Black Chuck introduced me. Julia, I asked them to do this."

He just looked at me, like I was supposed to fill in the blank. But I didn't want to. My mind was darting to places that scared me, so I kept silent, waiting for him to go on.

"Julia . . . I asked them to jump me in."

No way. He had to be playing. Eric was so much smarter, so much more mature than any guy I knew. There was no way he'd join a gang. Eric came to Brooklyn to start over.

He searched my eyes. "Aren't you gonna say something?"

"This is a grimey joke, Eric."

"It's not a joke."

Okay. So it wasn't a joke.

"Then it's *fucked up!*"

He looked startled. "Calm down. Look, I knew you wouldn't like it, but you've gotta understand—this is what I want."

"Was it Black Chuck who convinced you?"

"Black Chuck had nothing to do with it. Actually, he was mad worried about how you'd react. But I knew where I should be. This is gonna take time to get used to, Julia. But if you can accept Black Chuck as a Crip, then you can accept me."

"It's not the same. He's not my boyfriend."

"C'mon, Julia. You see things too black and white. These Crips are good guys. They're like a family. I got nothing in this city. Why shouldn't I have buddies?"

This wasn't Eric talking. Those words couldn't be coming out of his mouth.

"You're a follower," I said. "I never thought you needed colors to tell you who you are."

"I don't. You act like you know everything, Julia. But there's a helluva lot of shit going on that you know nothing about. So don't preach at me."

"Preach at you? You know how I feel about gangs!"

"Yeah, and two of your best friends are in gangs. What does that say?"

"*That's* not the point. If you really cared about me, you would've talked to me about this before getting jumped in."

"I knew what you'd say, and I wanted to make this decision on my own. I'm asking you to respect that. You don't need to have anything to do with the Crips. Can't you see past that and be with me?"

"I can't, Eric. You know I can't." I started to walk away, then stopped. "Just answer one question. Why? You really did it just to have buddies?"

He dropped his eyes. "Back in Detroit, I was Crip."

It was like a blow to my gut.

He was Crip the whole time.

I didn't go back to class that afternoon. Screw it.

I held back tears the whole bus ride home. Once I got to my apartment, I burst like a dam. It felt like something in my chest had been ripped out. Now there was just a gaping hole.

All my instincts had made me think that Eric would never get involved in a gang. I hadn't even worried about him hanging around with Black Chuck. Little did I know it was like putting a bottle of vodka in front of a recovering alcoholic.

Was this my fault? Would Eric have stayed square if I hadn't introduced him to Black Chuck?

I doubted it. Eric didn't regret joining the FJC. He'd made it clear that he hadn't been pressured into it. But why would he want that kind of life? When you joined a gang, sure, you had new friends, but you also had new enemies in the rival gangs. Why would anyone want that kind of drama?

If he'd planned to join the FJC all along, I didn't see why

he hadn't gone for a Crip girl. Why go for me when he knew I had no love for gangs?

I ran out of tissue so I started using toilet paper. The tears kept coming. I missed Eric already. But how could I go out with him when he stood for everything I hated?

He was a gangbanger. A follower. And he'd kept me in the dark so I wouldn't try to talk him out of joining. That said a lot. Eric *knew* how I would feel and didn't care.

Our relationship was over. OVER. Three weeks of bliss, then my world came crashing down.

His loss. Definitely his loss.

So why did it hurt so much?

After a while I stopped crying, grabbed some pretzels and switched on the TV. Some skinny white guy was talking to dead people. It made me think about my mom. Tears filled my eyes again. Wasn't it at times like this that a girl needed her mom?

I almost jumped out of my skin when the apartment buzzer rang.

Was it Eric?

Should I answer it?

After the second buzz, I did. "Hello?"

"Julia!"

Q.

"Come on up."

I waited with the door half-open. When she saw me, her eyes widened. "Julia, what's wrong?"

"Eric joined the FJC," I said, plunking down on the couch.

"Oh my God. Are you serious? That explains why his face was so messed up today. Why'd he do it?"

"Apparently he was a Crip back in Detroit. I guess that's why his mom sent him here in the first place."

"And he didn't even tell you? That asshole!"

"Yeah. So I broke up with him."

"Of course you did! You don't want to be with somebody like that. You deserve the best."

I sniffed. "I really thought he wasn't the type to join a gang."

"You don't think Black Chuck pressured him into it, do you?"

"Don't get me started on Black Chuck. He shouldn't have brought Eric to meet his friends."

"To be fair, maybe Eric wanted to meet them."

"Black Chuck could've said *no*. He knew how I'd feel!"

"If Eric wanted to join, he would've done it anyway, with or without Black Chuck's help."

"I know. How am I going to face Eric in class every day?"

"Easy. You don't give him the time of day."

LOW

As it turned out, I shouldn't have been worried about seeing Eric in class. He didn't show up at school for the rest of the week. No doubt it was the influence of his new crew.

He'd told me that he wanted to graduate, but if he kept this up, he wouldn't have a chance.

Well, that was his problem, not mine.

"*Psst*. Julia." The kid sitting across from me pointed at the back door of the classroom.

Black Chuck was there, waving at me through the glass. I put up my hand to ask for the bathroom pass.

He was waiting for me around the corner in the stairwell. The air smelled of a recent spliff.

"What up, Ju? You didn't call me back."

"I didn't feel like talking."

"Heard you and Eric broke up."

"I dumped him. Did he tell you that part?"

"Yeah."

"You must've figured I'd do that when you jumped him in."

"I'll be straight with you, Julia. That kid is as blue as they come. I didn't sell him on nothing."

"Did you try to talk him out of it, then?"

"Why would I do that? We need strong guys like him to get our backs."

"If you're so worried about your back, you should get out, not bring more people in." I shook my head. He wasn't going to listen to that. "Your crew needed Eric, hunh? What about me? I needed him too."

"I'm sure you can get him back if you want."

"But I don't want to date a gang member! You don't get me, do you? After we've been friends so long, you don't even get me?"

"You're wrong, Ju. I do get you. Believe it or not, I didn't really want Eric to join. But after Scrap met him I couldn't do nothing about it. Sure, Eric's a cool guy. But you and me? We tight. I didn't want to hurt you."

"You did." My eyes filled with tears. I sat down on the step beside him. He put his arm around me.

I wiped my eyes. "If you could just wake up one day, be in another city, with all new people and none of this Crip stuff, would you do it?"

He didn't say anything for a long time. I thought maybe he hadn't heard me, or the question had pissed him off. Then he said, real quiet, "Maybe."

"Eric had a chance to start over, and he didn't take it. Why didn't he take it?"

"I don't know. Why don't you ask him?"

"I don't want to talk to him."

"That's up to you. I always pictured you going out with one of those Honors guys anyway."

"Are you serious?"

"Mad serious. You're the smartest girl I know. You need a guy who'll go to college. You're gonna be a famous poet someday, Julia."

"You really think so? But you haven't even read any of my stuff."

"I read some stuff here and there. Remember that poem about your mom?"

"That was in seventh grade!"

"Yeah, well, I knew you had it in you. Point is, you can be friends with peeps like me and Eric, but you oughta get yourself a better boyfriend."

"*Chuck!*" a security guard shouted from the top of the stairs. "What are you doing here? You're on suspension!"

"Gotta bounce." Black Chuck jumped up and ran down the hall. The security guard bolted down the stairs and headed after him.

Every night I hoped Eric would call.

It made no sense. I was the one who dumped him, so why should he call me?

And what could he possibly say? *I changed my mind you were right I asked them to jump me out of the gang can we be together again?* Even if he'd changed his mind about joining—even if, somehow, he realized that he'd made a mistake—there was no turning back and he knew it.

Life went back to "normal." I wasn't falling asleep in class anymore because I wasn't staying up past midnight IM'ing with Eric.

I wasn't late for any classes.

Life was back to normal. Aka *boring*.

Love
A house of cards, stacked so perfectly
So still
So fragile
Cold wind, Reality
Blows it down
Rips you apart
The death of dreams.

The Note

.

Monday, Eric was back in class.

"Long time, eh?" he said, dark eyes touching my face. "How's it going?"

I felt a lump in my throat. He still had an effect on me, damn him. I looked down at my desk. "I'm good. You?"

"A'ight."

A crisp voice said from the front of the classroom, "Eric, come here, please."

I couldn't hear the conversation between Eric and Ms. Ivey, but her nostrils flared, which meant she was pissed. She was obviously telling him that he'd better explain his absences if he was going to have a chance at passing the class.

Eventually she flicked her wrist for him to go to his seat. Eric shrugged like he didn't care.

The class went by way too slow. I could feel the heat of Eric's stare on my back. Halfway through the class he tried to pass me a note, but I didn't take it. With my luck, Ms. Ivey would catch me reading it. He might not care about passing the class, but I did.

When the bell rang, he was the first one out of his seat. He dropped the note on my desk and walked out.

I picked up my books and left the class, stopping in the hallway to read the note.

The three words made my heart ache.

MISS YOU DIVINE.

"What did he mean by that?" I asked Q. We were on the crowded, rank-smelling bus home, hanging on to a pole at the back.

Q shot a dirty look at some kids who'd bumped her as they squeezed by. "He means he misses you."

"You know what I mean. Why bother telling me? He knows I'm not taking him back."

"Be ready, Julia. He might try to play you again. Don't get sucked in."

"I won't."

She tapped the metal pole with an acrylic nail. "I think you need to find yourself a rebound."

"Got anybody in mind?"

"Not exactly. But a rebound is easy to find if you're in the right place. And you will be." She took a pink flyer out of her jacket pocket and handed it to me.

It's **FLY FRIDAY** at the Lava Lounge.
Music by DJ Mo Flow.
Ladies Free. Men $10 B4 midnight, $20 after.
Shout-Out to All of Brooklyn.
No flags, no colors.

"Fly Friday, huh? Sounds good. Who else is going?"

"The entire football team, honey. The *entire* football team."

CHOICES

I spent the rest of the week prepping for Fly Friday.

Tuesday: Went to King's Plaza to get a new outfit.

Wednesday: Went to Canal Street after school to get a striped Kate Spade knockoff to match my outfit.

Thursday: Got a manicure at the Korean place down the block.

Friday: Got Marlise to blow out my hair. Borrowed Q's kicks.

I started doing my makeup half an hour before Q was set to come over. On the bathroom counter was a copy of *Elle* magazine with step-by-step instructions on how to get the smoky eye look I'd seen on my favorite celebs. Armed with black eyeliner, I drew a thick line under my eyes, then smudged it with a Q-tip.

When I was done, I took a step back.

I looked like a dead prom queen.

So much for that idea. I cleaned up my eyes and settled on my usual brown eyeliner and mascara.

My lips were easier to do. I liked the JLo shiny-lipped style. First, the liner, then the natural pink lipstick, followed by a few layers of shiny gloss. Perfect.

After my makeup was done, I put on my new black-and-white cami and black velvet pants.

Q showed up looking beautiful as usual. Girly stuff came more naturally to her than to me. She had a way of looking elegant 24-7. Tonight the color was orange—earrings, cap, scarf, shirt, shoes, even the embroidery on her jeans. She managed to put hot outfits together without dropping much money because she knew all of the best deals in Flatbush.

When we arrived at the Lava Lounge, a doorman frisked us. He was thorough enough that I giggled, but cute enough that I didn't mind.

The lounge was packed. At the far end, there were couches and low tables with tea lights. Closer to us was the club part, with a spacious dance floor lined with mirrors. The first sweep of my eyes took in a lot of cute guys. Too bad I kept thinking about one in particular.

"Girls!" Marie ran up, hugging us. She was rocking her Blood colors, which didn't impress me. The flyer specifically said: *No flags, No colors.* By the looks of things, Marie wasn't the only one.

"The Bitches here?" Q asked Marie.

"'Course they are. The Niggaz too. I'm gonna get some ass tonight. That's a promise."

"Maybe you can set Julia up with some ass," Q said. "Non–gang member ass."

"I don't know any of that kind." Marie looked over her shoulder. "My Bitches are calling me. Are you girls sure you don't want to join the RLB? I'd love it if we could all be one big group. Julia, don't you think it would be a great way of getting back at Eric if you joined?"

Marie just didn't get it. I shook my head, not bothering to explain.

Marie went back to her Bitches and we headed to the bar, ordering two Incredible Hulks. The cute bartender asked if we were twenty-one. We both said yes. He smiled and served us.

By the end of our first drink we were on the dance floor breaking out our moves. We saw some girls we knew from school, so we joined them.

I did a doubletake when I spotted Eric walk past the dance floor. He was with two Crips from our school, Hex and Rolo.

"What is he doing here?" Q shouted.

"I don't care!" I shouted back.

We watched the blue crew walk right past a group of RLN. Somebody must have shouted something, because Eric's head whipped back. For a second, I thought they were going to fight. But Eric and his crew kept walking, thank God.

"That was close," I said to Q. "Did you see that?"

She nodded.

Determined to forget about him, I focused on my moves. He had no business distracting me when I was trying to have a good time and find a rebound.

When Ciara came on, people flooded onto the dance floor. Time to kick it up a notch. We made a circle, Q and me winding it up in the middle. I could feel Eric's stare all over me. I danced sensually, wanting him to know what he was missing. But I refused to look in his direction.

So much for a rebound tonight. With Eric around, how could I think of anybody else?

On the good side, Q found herself a guy to dance with. I

backed off the dance floor and went to the bar for a drink. Ice water, this time. Leaning my elbow on the bar, I was careful not to look in Eric's direction.

"I can't believe that asshole had the balls to come here!" It was Marie. "And then to rock his colors right in front of Naquan!"

"Who's Naquan?"

"Head of the Real Live Niggaz, baby! Eric walked right past him like it ain't nothing. He's gonna get it."

"What, you plan to teach him a lesson?"

"Not me. He's gonna get jumped on his way out of here. Naquan wants to really fuck up his pretty face. I bet you'll be glad to see that, hunh? After the way that Crab punk played you!"

"Uh, yeah. He deserves it."

"You said it." She walked away.

Oh my God. They were really going to hurt Eric.

He only had two guys to back him up. From what I'd seen, there were at least a dozen RLN in the bar, and that didn't include whoever might be outside.

I couldn't let it happen. I just couldn't.

I asked the bartender if he had something to write with.

He passed me a pen. On a napkin, I wrote:

RLN are planning to jump you outside.
Find another way out.

I folded the napkin and walked toward him. He spotted me when I was halfway there.

Oh Eric, how did you get yourself into this mess?

I stopped in front of him, my heart pounding.

"Hi, Eric."

"Hey, Divine."

I grabbed his hand and squeezed it. His hand closed around the note. "Hope you're having a good time," I said.

"You too."

I felt his eyes follow me as I walked away. I headed toward the girls' bathroom at the back of the bar, and reapplied lip gloss in front of the mirror.

How the hell is he going to get out of this?

When I left the bathroom, Eric was there, flicking closed his cell phone.

I stopped dead, pinned by his eyes.

"Thanks," he said.

"What are you going to do?"

"Take care of it."

"Don't do anything stupid, Eric."

"Don't sweat it." He stepped out of my way, letting me pass him in the narrow hallway. As I walked by, I caught the scent of his cologne.

God, I missed him.

Back in the lounge, I found Q at the bar with some girl-friends.

"Julia, where'd you go?"

"Bathroom." I couldn't tell her the whole story, not with the rest of the girls around. "Where's the guy?"

"One girl wasn't enough for him. I cut him loose when he grabbed Shavelle and tried to get us to sandwich him. Sicko." She checked her watch. "I'm done with this place. Wanna get a bite?"

"Let's stay a bit longer," I said. "Some more hot guys came in." I didn't want to leave until I knew Eric got out safe.

Q yawned. "Okay. We'll stay long enough for you to get your rebound kiss. Who's it gonna be?"

Over the next half hour, I made eyes at a few guys, more to satisfy Q than anything else. She had no clue that I was stalling.

And then it happened. Eric, Rolo, and Hex left the bar. Naquan and his Bloods, I knew, would be waiting for them.

Suddenly a crowd of people rushed toward the door. Something had started outside. I pushed to the front of the pack, losing Q. I had to see what was happening.

A wave of people pushed behind me, thrusting me out onto the curb. A huge fight was blocking the sidewalk. There were at least twenty people scrapping.

Eric had called the Crips for backup. Smart move.

I caught sight of Eric somewhere in the middle of the brawl. He was on his feet, holding his own. And there was somebody else I recognized—Scrap, Black Chuck's big brother. Tall and muscular with crazy braids flying everywhere, Scrap fought like a savage.

It felt like only seconds passed before I heard the sirens. Abandoning the fight, people ran off in every direction. Cop cars barreled down Smith Street, stopping in front of the bar.

By then, it was too late to make arrests. There were a couple of Bloods on the ground, too beat up to run. One of the cops radioed for ambulances.

I closed my eyes and sighed, relieved. Eric was going to be okay.

For tonight, anyway.

THE CALL

A loud buzzing jolted me out of a dream.

I slapped my alarm clock, but it didn't stop the buzzing.

I finally realized it was the phone.

Grabbing for it, I said, "Hello?"

"Bitch!" a female voice screamed in my ear.

Then a dial tone.

Redemption

The phone rang again at 11:53 a.m. By that time, I'd almost convinced myself that it was time to drag my ass out of bed.

"Hello?"

"Hey. It's Eric."

I cleared my throat. "Uh, hi."

"You're just waking up?"

"Yeah."

"I figured I should wait till noon."

"Yeah."

"I really want to see you, Julia. We need to talk."

"About what?"

"About everything. Is your dad home?"

"No, but—"

"Can I come over?"

"I don't think so."

I heard him blow air into the phone. "I'm not a thug, Julia. You can trust me."

It wasn't him I didn't trust.

It was me. I had a major soft spot for Eric.

Or maybe a blind spot.

"I'll see you, just not here. How about Hal's?"

"Okay. What time?"

"Twelve thirty."

"Sure. See you then."

"Later."

I hung up.

This could be a mistake. I knew I didn't have much resistance where Eric was concerned. But I just couldn't pass up the chance to see him.

I missed him so much.

Hal's was a greasy spoon around the corner from my building. I'd met Eric there a couple of times before.

Hal's decor was all about the man himself. The walls were covered with black-and-white photos—Hal as a boy, a teen, a middle-aged man—packing on more and more pounds. The last picture had Hal with his wife, grown children, and first grandchild; there were no pictures of Hal after that, because he died of a heart attack. Hal's "home-cooking" finally caught up with him.

Eric was already sitting at a table with a soda when I got there. I noticed he had a black eye and a cut lip from last night's fight.

Didn't make him any less beautiful.

I sat down across from him. He was about to say something when the waiter showed up and handed me a menu. When he left, I looked at Eric, expecting him to start.

"I owe you my life, Julia. Last night would've turned out real bad if you hadn't warned me." He reached across the table for my hand. I let him take it, though I was uncomfortable. I didn't want to believe that I'd saved his life. It terrified me.

"I'm sorry you think I played you, Julia. I know you're not gonna forgive me, but I want you to know that I'm not who you think I am."

"You're not a gangbanger?"

"That isn't what I mean. You thought I didn't care how you felt about me joining the gang. I *did* care. There was just nothing I could do about it."

"What are you saying—they forced you to join?"

"No. I *already* joined in Detroit and I was never officially jumped out. The way I see it, I just moved from one set to another."

"Have you looked in the mirror? That gash you have on your face is red, Eric. Your blood isn't blue." I pushed my menu away. "We don't get each other, so there's no point in talking about this."

He caught my wrist. "Wait, *please*. I'm not done."

I sat back. "Go ahead."

"I need to know why you warned me last night. If you hate my guts, why did you help me?"

"I don't hate you, Eric. I didn't wanna see you get hurt."

The waiter came up to take our orders. Did I really want to stay?

Eric saw me hesitate. "C'mon, Julia. It's just lunch." He looked at the waiter. "All-day breakfast, please."

I gave the waiter back my menu. "Me too."

When the waiter left, I said, "So this is why you wanted to meet up with me—to thank me?"

He nodded. "To buy you lunch."

"For saving your life."

"Yeah."

"You're getting off easy. Don't you think saving your life deserves someplace better than Hal's? Like Tavern on the Green?"

He smiled. "That's my Divine."

"Please don't call me that."

"Why not? We're still friends, right?"

"Friends? I don't see it. I'm an all-or-nothing type of girl."

"I'll take *all*, then." His eyes looked hopeful. My insides twisted.

"It can't work, Eric. You've never been straight with me. I was really into you, and there was this whole side of you that you purposely kept from me."

He was quiet for a long time. I guess my words had some impact.

He suddenly said, "You're right."

"I am?"

"I didn't think I needed to be open with you. Most people I meet don't ask me a lot of questions about my past. They don't want to know. But you're not like other people."

"If *other people* don't care if you're straight with them or not, then I guess I'm different. But I think there are lots of people like me, you just don't hang out with them. Look around at your Crip brothers and sisters. They're trash-talkers, hunh? All they talk about is who's on your territory, who they're gonna jump, who they're gonna hustle."

"Any one of them would take a bullet for me. That's what matters."

"Who says I wouldn't take a bullet for you? Not because I'm Crip, but because I'm—I *was*—your girlfriend."

"I think you're sheltered, Julia. You don't act like you really know the streets."

"I do, trust me. I've seen a lot of stuff."

"But you haven't *lived* that stuff."

"I made a choice not to."

He shook his head. "You don't get it. No matter where I go, my gang, it's in me. They're all that's between me and a wooden box. You saw how they came to back me up last night. I can count on them. If my brother could've had that kind of backup . . ."

Brother? He had a brother?

A muscle bunched in his jaw. "They told him to run his pockets, but he didn't want to give up his cash and his phone. He wasn't scared of nothing." His eyes burned. "Bloods killed him. He was sixteen."

"God." Tears blurred my vision. I reached for his hand, but he pulled back, cracking his knuckles.

"He was my big brother. He always looked out for me. But he had nobody to get his back. I'd probably be dead too, if it wasn't for my Crip brothers in Detroit."

"I'm sorry, Eric."

"My mom sent me to a shrink after. She couldn't afford it, but she did it anyway. The guy was talking shit about moving on. Letting go. But it doesn't work like that. When I think of him, I always go back to the same place in my mind, where I'm fourteen, and he's my big brother. And then his friend comes in screaming."

"They say as time goes on, it doesn't hurt as bad," I said.

"That's what they say."

"So in the end, it's because of him that you joined the Crips."

"Yeah. I live to honor my brother, Julia. One day you'll understand that."

"I think I understand you better now."

I wanted to tell him how much I cared, how much I wanted to hold him, to comfort him. So I told him with my eyes.

And that's when his hand grasped mine, holding on tighter than ever.

* * *

After lunch we walked through Prospect Park. It was a gray day, but people still found reasons to go to the park. Soccer and football leagues were still going strong. Kids and their parents sailed mechanized boats in the big pond, getting a kick out of the rippling waves caused by the strong wind.

We held hands. I'd swear there was an electrical current passing between us. Eric must have felt it too. He was always finding reasons to touch me—brushing hair away from my face, making circles on my back. Anything to be closer.

Telling me about his brother had knocked down a wall between us. A lot made sense now. I finally knew where the darkness was coming from. And I understood why he'd joined the Crips in the first place, even if I wasn't sure he'd made the decision.

But if it had kept him alive in Detroit, wasn't it the right decision?

Yeah, and it had almost got him seriously fucked up last night.

Obviously the issue wasn't as clear-cut as I thought. And if it wasn't clear-cut, then maybe I shouldn't judge him for his decision.

I noticed he wasn't wearing his colors today. Was that for

me? Or maybe he just didn't wear them all the time?

We stopped to skip stones in the pond. Eric could skip a stone eight times. He tried to teach me how, even helping me pick out a perfect rock—a small, round, flat one. But I wasn't really listening to what he was teaching me—I was watching him. I could hardly stop myself from wrapping my arms around him and kissing his gorgeous mouth.

We sat down on a bench. I snuggled into his side, and he put his arm around me.

"Feels like this means something," he said.

I laid my cheek against the cool leather of his jacket. "I think so."

"I hope it doesn't mean that we're gonna be friends."

I smiled against his jacket. "Well . . ."

"Look at me, Julia. I'm serious."

I raised my head, feeling a little uncertain.

"You don't usually hold hands with your friends, do you?" I could see the insecurity in his eyes.

"No."

"Good, because I don't want to be friends with you. I want to be *with* you. Will you give me another chance?"

I couldn't say the *yes* I was feeling, not yet. "You aren't wearing your colors today. Is that because of me?"

"I thought you wouldn't be comfortable. Look, if we go out together, I won't wear my colors. But I'm gonna wear them with my crew and when I'm at school. Can you live with that?"

Could I live without *him*, was the question.

"I can live with that."

"I'm glad. God, I missed you, Divine!"

Bitch

"Come again?" A piece of egg from Q's bacon-egg-and-cheese fell out of her mouth. "You're *what?*"

We were on the bus Monday morning. I knew she'd be shocked by my news. I was shocked myself.

"We're back together. He called on Saturday saying that he really wanted to see me. He wanted to thank me for giving him the heads-up Friday night."

"Heads-up about what?"

I lowered my voice. "You know that fight outside the club? Marie told me the RLN were gonna jump Eric. So I warned him."

Q's eyes bugged out. "I can't believe you did that! What were you thinking? Does Marie know you warned him?"

"Probably. I got a call about four in the morning. Some girl yelled 'bitch' and then hung up."

I didn't like the worried look on Q's face. I'd been trying to contain my own anxiety since the crank call by focusing on Eric.

"So you warned Eric," she said. "How does that lead to you getting back together?"

"We went to lunch and we started talking. Really talking."

"What does that mean—you weren't talking before? You were just making out?"

"No, but before, he wasn't totally real with me. It's hard to explain. He told me stuff about his past that made me understand him better."

"Like what?"

"Like his brother got killed. And he wasn't even in a gang."

"Holy shit."

"Yeah. After hearing that, I couldn't blame Eric so much for joining."

"Why didn't he tell you that before?"

"He doesn't like to talk about it."

"Look, I don't mean to sound insensitive here, but what

happened to his brother doesn't mean he has to be Crip his whole life, does it?"

"I hope not."

"Just because you feel bad about his brother doesn't mean you should get back together with him. Even if you understand his reasons, that doesn't make it cool that he runs with the Crips."

"Maybe not, but Eric is the best guy I've ever met, and I'm not gonna judge him. It's easy for us to put people down for joining gangs—especially people like Marie who just join to get ass. But *some* people actually join for good reasons. Eric might not even be alive today if it weren't for his Crip buddies."

"You know what this means, right? You'll be Crip by association."

"No I won't. It'll be like with Black Chuck. I can hang out with him without having anything to do with the Crips."

"You'd better think about this, Julia. Sure, Eric got away from Naquan and the RLN Friday night, but do you want to be there the time he doesn't see it coming?"

"I'll risk it, I guess."

"Don't guess, Julia, *know*. I don't think it's worth it. Are you sure this is what you want?"

"Yeah."

"Your choice." She took another bite of her sandwich.

We got off the bus, stopping at a deli to buy drinks and gum. When we came out, Marie and three RLB were on the sidewalk. I knew immediately that they'd been waiting for us. For me.

Marie's hands were on her hips. "Tell me straight up, Julia. You told Eric he was gonna get jumped, didn't you?"

"No."

"Liar." Marie's Bitch-friend, Toneya, stepped up beside her.

"You're the only one outside the gang who knew," Marie said, her lips barely moving.

Her coldness caught me off guard. I knew Marie to be loud and mouthy when she got mad, not like this. Marie wouldn't hurt me, would she? We'd been friends since junior high!

But she had her Bitches with her. Did she have something to prove?

"Marie, I don't want trouble," I said. "Eric isn't stupid. He must've figured that Naquan was gonna try something."

Q said, "Chill, girls. Julia's no rat." She grabbed my arm and urged me across the street.

"Are they coming after us?" I asked, afraid to look back.

Q glanced over her shoulder. "No, but let's hurry in case they change their minds."

"Marie won't start something, will she?"

"You know her as well as I do. She can be a pit bull when she wants to be. I'll talk to her. In the meantime, watch your back."

"I will."

"Good morning, Divine."

Eric was waiting for me at my locker where I dropped off my coat and book bag every morning. He pulled me close and kissed me, not caring who was watching.

"You taste good," he said against my lips.

"That's Scope for you."

"Are we gonna hang out after school?"

"Depends. Will you wait for me till the end of ninth?"

"Sure. Where do you want to meet?"

"Anywhere. We'll talk about it in History."

"I've been meaning to tell you, I'm not going back to that class."

"Why not? You were doing good, weren't you?"

"Yeah, but I missed so much class, Ivey's gonna fail me anyway."

"Not necessarily. Trust me, go back to class."

"There's no point. Anyway, I'll see you later."

"Okay. Later."

The morning went by fast. Everybody was asking questions about Eric and me getting back together. I guess people saw our morning kiss, and news spread like bird flu around here.

There was a lot of talk about the fight Friday night. Bloods and Crips were vowing revenge against one another. But then, what's new?

Sixth-period American History rolled around. I felt bad about Eric not coming back to class. True, he'd cut a lot of classes, but maybe if he showed up from now on Ms. Ivey would pass him. I felt partly responsible for him not showing up. If I hadn't been so cold when we broke up, maybe he wouldn't have felt like he had to avoid me.

When the bell rang ending the class, I went up to Ms. Ivey. She looked exhausted, but she managed a smile. "Yes?"

"Um, Eric Valienté thinks that he doesn't have a chance of passing this class. Is that true?"

She raised her eyebrows. "It should be Eric talking to me about this, not you."

"Yeah, but the thing is, he thinks he has no chance, so he's not going to bother. The reason he didn't come to class was because of me—we'd been going out and we broke up."

"But you're back together now?"

"Uh, yeah." I smiled a little.

Ms. Ivey wasn't smiling. "I'll be honest with you. I'm not sure that you and Eric Valienté are suited to each other."

"Why?"

"You're a very intelligent girl, Julia. With a little extra effort, you could be in Advanced Placement classes. Eric doesn't take school very seriously."

"I know he wants to do better."

Ms. Ivey stood up, saying good-bye to a couple of students. Then she said, "I'm not blind, Julia. Eric's a gang member. I recognize the colors. I won't lecture you on the implications of that; you probably know far more about such things than I do. I'm just surprised at your judgment."

My face reddened. I was speechless.

"You're a wonderful young woman," she said, as if it softened the blow. "I don't want to put you on the defensive. In answer to your question, tell Eric that if he doesn't cut class again and completes all of his homework, he has a chance of passing."

"I'll tell him," I said, relieved. "He'll be back in class tomorrow."

THE LOCKER ROOM

"Stretch, more, more!" Ms. Russo stood over me as I sat on the mat, straining to touch my toes. "Keep working on that flexibility, Julia."

"Yeah," I grumbled. I loved dancing, but all this stretching was ridiculous. I'd never pulled anything when I danced at home or at parties.

Next we had to cross our legs, putting our feet over our thighs. I closed my eyes and placed my hands on my knees, palms upward.

"Breathe in, breathe out," Ms. Russo said.

After the stretching was finished, we were on our feet for two warm-up laps around the gym, then we got into rows. Ms. Russo switched on the music and told us to follow her moves.

Ms. Russo was cool. She didn't teach us Modern Dance like you'd see at some dance show at BAM. She taught us the kind of moves you could use at parties. The course should've really been called Hip-Hop Dancing, but I guess she couldn't sell that to the principal.

Five minutes before the end of the period, Ms. Russo dismissed us so we could change. It was always a rush in the change room, at least for those of us who didn't want to be late for our next class. While I was opening my combination lock, I noticed a sudden silence around me.

I looked to my right. Marie was standing there with three Bitches: Toneya, Lisa, and Marta.

"What's up?" Cold sweat pitted my underarms.

"We know you snitched," Marie said, cracking her gum. "And you know what they say about snitches?"

Snitches get stitches.

"C'mon, Marie. We're cool, right?"

She advanced on me.

In the next few seconds I knew three things:

1. I was backed into the lockers and had nowhere to run.

2. These girls didn't fight solo. It was four against one.

3. Nobody would be brave enough to help me.

They came at me like chaos.

I managed to dodge the first punch, which connected with the locker. "Fuck!" Marie shouted.

They pushed forward, slamming me against the lockers. My head snapped back, a metallic thud resounding through my skull.

Blows rained down everywhere. Too many to block. I hoisted my arms to try to protect my head.

"Whore!"

"Skank!"

"Snitch!"

A whole crowd was watching, dragging friends in from the hallway. I could hear them cheering.

I felt every blow—a fist in my jaw, my shoulder, a steel-toed boot in my shin. I felt their spit on my face. I felt a wad of gum pressed into my hair.

What the fuck are they doing to me?

I lashed back, tearing through the maze of fists and smashing someone's face. They caught my right arm and held it against the steel of the locker, giving Marie free rein. I fought to lift my left arm to shield my face—they pinned that, too.

I wanted to scream, but it got garbled in my throat as Marie smashed my face and chest. I tried to crouch down, but somebody pulled me up by the hair and hit my face. I tasted blood.

I knew I'd been hit by Marie's gold-plated name ring.

I managed to free my right arm to sink a hard jab into somebody's tit.

I wriggled down to the floor, trying to crouch under the bench. Another blow to my head. The lights started to go out. They were going to kill me. They weren't stopping, even though I was down, helpless.

I heard security guards shouting. The blows stopped.

I wasn't conscious when the guards found me. I later heard they were worried that I was dead.

They weren't the only ones.

SURFACE

"Julia?" Dad was standing over me, tears in his eyes.

"Am I okay?" I asked him shakily.

"You'll be all right. How do you feel?"

"Achy. Dizzy."

"You have a concussion, so they're going to keep you overnight."

"Where's here?" I looked around without moving my head too much.

"New York Presbyterian."

"How long . . . ?"

"A few hours. You had some visitors. Eric and Black Chuck were here."

"They're gone?"

"The doctor thought you shouldn't be disturbed tonight. Tomorrow you can come home. They're going to wake you up a few times in the night to make sure you're okay."

"Why?"

"When people have concussions, it's important to keep a close eye on them."

"Is it okay if I go back to sleep now?"

"Of course."

I squeezed his hand. "Will you stay with me till I fall asleep?"

"Sure, bella. I'll be right here."

In the darkness, I felt a hand on my shoulder, shaking me. I groaned, but eventually opened my eyes to find a nurse looking down at me. "Doing all right, Julia?"

"Yeah."

"Good, then. Go back to sleep now."

She left, but I was still awake. Dad wasn't there to hold my hand. The room was dark and silent except for breathing at other corners of the room. It sounded like there were two or three other people in here.

My bladder was going to burst. I didn't think I could survive much longer without going to the bathroom. Slowly, I swung my legs out of bed, my bare feet touching the cold floor. Holding on to the railing, I stood up. My head swam a little, but I knew I could make it. It was kind of like being drunk.

I shuffled across the room, closing the bathroom door behind me before flicking the light on. I pulled up my hospital gown and sat on the toilet.

The sight of purple bruises on my thighs and arms sent a shock wave through me. I peeked down the front of my hospital gown to find dark splotches all over my chest and stomach.

Oh God.

How could they do this to me? Those girls hardly even knew me. And Marie . . . she was supposed to be my friend.

I sobbed quietly, smothering the noise with my hands.

When I was finished on the toilet, I got up to wash my hands and saw my reflection in the mirror. I had two black eyes, a swollen lip, and a bandage on my cheek.

Is that me?

The next morning, Dad was there when I woke up.

The nurse helped me get dressed and brought me downstairs to where he was parked. I got in the car carefully, but it didn't stop my body from screaming in pain.

"Did you take the day off?" I asked as he swung the old Ford into traffic.

"I tried. I only managed to switch to the late shift."

"Sorry."

"You're not the one who should be sorry. Whoever did this to you will be sorry. Your school contacted the police. They want you to make a statement at some point. You should also take some pictures of your injuries when you get home."

"I'm not talking to the cops, Dad, so don't bother. If I get them involved, I get called a snitch and a punk. Then everybody sees me as an easy target."

"So what are you gonna do then? Just let them get away with it?"

"I haven't thought about it yet."

"I think we should press charges," he insisted.

"Even if we did, it wouldn't be worth the trouble. Getting into a fight doesn't get you in juvey."

"I didn't think it was a fight. From what I heard, it was an *attack*."

I couldn't argue with that. I hadn't had a goddamn chance to fight back.

"I want you out of that school, Julia. I don't like the kind of people there; I never did. We'll get you a safety transfer."

"I'm not transferring."

"Why not?"

"Because I don't run from my problems."

"What the hell are you talking about? You wouldn't be running from anything. Don't you think you'd be more comfortable if you didn't have to share the hallways with the people who did this to you?"

"I'd look like a punk if I left."

"Do you care that much what people think that you'll put your safety at risk?"

"I don't wanna change schools, Dad. I like where I'm at. I'm not gonna let what happened make me have to leave. That's what the Bitches who jumped me want." I looked at him. "I haven't forgotten the stories you told me about growing up in Astoria. It was rough, but you got by. So let me deal with this, okay?"

"I had no idea you were this hardheaded."

"What did you expect? I'm your daughter."

He sighed. "Okay, you got me there. But if they so much as look at you again, you're getting that safety transfer."

"I hear you, Dad."

ABANDON

When I got home, I checked the messages on my cell.

Messages from Q, Eric, and Black Chuck.

Called Eric's cell. No answer. Black Chuck's cell. No answer.

Q didn't have a cell. I'd have to talk to her when she got home from school.

School.

A flash of the locker room hit me. I closed my eyes and curled my fists.

Bitches.

Would pay.

With pain.

I spent the day watching talk shows. Dad left for work at four.

Soon after I heard the buzz.

I answered, "Who is it?"

"It's Q."

When she appeared in the doorway, she looked me over. Her eyes misted up. "Can I hug you?"

"Lightly."

She put her arms around me, careful not to squeeze.

"Have you talked to Eric or Black Chuck yet?" she asked.

"I couldn't get them on their cells."

"That's because they were busy."

"What do you mean?"

"Sit down, Julia."

We went to the couch. I eased myself down.

"If you've been plotting revenge, you don't have to worry. Your Crip friends took care of it. Guess who got jumped after school at the bus stop?"

My eyes widened.

"Yep, the Bitches who attacked you. By, like, ten Crip girls. Marie's face got cut. We saw the whole thing from across the street. Black Chuck and Eric must've put them up to it."

"I can't believe it. I hardly know the Crip girls."

"I'm sure it didn't take much convincing. There's been a lot of tension around the school lately. It's all-out war now."

I pictured the scene. The Bitches got jumped! A feeling of satisfaction went through me.

"Where are the girls?" I asked. "They didn't wanna stop by?"

Q's eyes flickered, and I knew something was coming.

"They hate what Marie did, Julia. But . . . they're all too afraid to say anything to her."

"What about you? You didn't say anything to her either?"

Her eyes dropped. "You know how she is."

No way. She could not be saying that.

I stared at her. "Look what she did to me! Are you that much of a punk that you can't even stand up for your best friend?"

"Don't call me a punk, Julia. This isn't *my* fault. If you hadn't gone out with a Crip, none of this would've happened. I told you it was impossible to stay neutral, but you didn't listen. Didn't you realize what would happen when you interfered with their plans to jump Eric?"

"What the fuck was I supposed to do—let Eric get jumped by a group of Bloods? Would you let that happen to someone you cared about? What if it were me?"

"I would've done the same as you—I hope. But I never would've been in that position in the first place. Look, Julia, I hate Marie for what she did to you. But no, I'm not gonna tell her that. At least I'm being honest with you. The other girls were too afraid to even come and see you."

"Thanks for being so goddamn brave then. What about when I'm back at school? Are you even gonna talk to me?"

She took a breath. "When you're back at school, me and the girls will keep our distance. Marie said we had to choose—her or you. But it really wasn't a choice, because she made it clear that if we didn't stick with her, we'd be on the RLB hit list."

"You're all ditching me because she's threatening you?"

"I told you, we don't have a choice. If we go up against Marie, we'll get jumped."

I couldn't believe what I was hearing. My friends were afraid to know me.

I started to cry. "I thought you were g-gonna stick by me. How could you p-pretend we're not friends anymore?"

She teared up too. "You're always gonna be my best friend. We just have to keep it quiet until after graduation. We can still talk on the phone and IM each other."

"But it's not the same, Q!"

"I know."

Yeah, her tears were real. But I also knew she blamed me for all of this. It was all my fault for going out with Eric. It was all my fault for not playing by the rules of survival we'd made up for ourselves.

Fuck those rules. We made them up in seventh grade, when we were sheltered and didn't know anything about the real world. Fuck basing all my decisions on what's safe, what will keep me out of trouble. She could live that way—I wasn't going to.

Q got up. She wasn't even gonna stay to comfort me or eat Doritos. "Maybe you're right, Julia. Maybe I am a punk. I'm just not a fighter, you know?"

"I get it."

What I got was:

I'd lost my best friend.

I'd lost my girlfriends.

All I had now was Eric and Black Chuck.

And a Crip debt to be paid.

Eric showed up soon after. Knowing all about rib injuries, he didn't try to hug me, he just touched my face. His eyes said everything. "Hey, boo."

"Good to see you."

"Got you some supplies." He slung off his backpack and unloaded chocolate almonds, ice cream, yogurt, and all that good stuff. "You need anything else, let me know."

"You're sweet. Come sit with me."

On the couch, I rested my head in the crook of his shoulder. I told myself I could handle anything as long as I had Eric with me.

We stayed like that for a while, not speaking. The sound of his breathing soothed me, like his hand stroking my hair.

"You don't know how sorry I am, Julia. I know it's my fault they went after you, because of what you did for me. I wish I could erase it, but I know I can't."

"I heard what you did, getting those Crip girls to jump them."

"Yeah, it had to be done. Justice, you know. It doesn't change that you got hurt because of me."

I lifted my head to look at him. "It's not your fault. I don't regret warning you, not for one second. And I don't regret that we're back together. Do you?"

"If I knew this was gonna happen . . ."

"Don't talk like that! I need you totally with me right now. We're together a hundred percent, right?"

"Yeah. I just wish I could've protected you." Raw emotion hardened his features. "I was ready to go after them myself, Julia. I was *this* close. Chuck talked me down, convinced me to let the girls do it."

"I know what you mean. I never thought I was a fighter, but when they jumped me, I felt this rage—like I could tear them up. But there were four of them, and they had me cornered. I didn't even have a chance to fight back—that was the worst part." I had a flash of memory of their faces and fists. I pushed it back. I couldn't go to that place of rage and helplessness, not now. Maybe not ever.

"The Crip girls did a good job. The Bitches were down for the count."

"You watched the whole thing?"

"We all did. Your friends were there too."

"They're not my friends anymore. Q was just over. She said they're all too scared to stand up to Marie, so they won't have anything to do with me. She said we could still talk on the phone. Yeah, whatever."

"What the fuck? She came over here to tell you that— when you're in this kinda shape?"

"They're all so scared of getting jumped that they sold me out. I don't give a shit anymore. Who needs friends like that?"

"I know, but you and Q, you were mad close. I'm sorry."

"Yeah, well. She's not who I thought she was. If she'd been in the locker room yesterday, I don't even think she would've tried to help me."

"You don't know that for sure."

"I know, Eric. In my gut, I know."

LIFE CHANGES FAST

I walked back into the school one week later.

Eric held my hand. With him, I could face anyone or anything.

Even enter a war zone.

I wasn't under any illusions. I knew who my friends were now. They weren't who they used to be.

There were no calls from my girls asking how I was doing. Not even an IM or an e-mail.

Years of friendship gone to hell.

But Eric had been over every night. And Black Chuck had stopped by a bunch of times. They were there for me. They took care of me.

"They're here," Eric said.

"Who?"

"You know who. Be nice, okay?"

"I'm always nice."

Sarah Stanley and Nessa Henriquez came up to us. Sarah was tall and dark-skinned, with perfect makeup and a curvy figure. Nessa was a small, fiery Dominican with glossy black curls. They threw their arms around Eric, kissing his cheeks. I felt a stab of jealousy. What did I expect? They called themselves family, didn't they?

"Sarah, Nessa, this is my girl, Julia."

"We kicked some fat ass for you last week," Nessa said. "Bet you're sorry you ever hung around with Marie."

"Yeah. Thanks for . . . helping out."

"It's cool," Sarah said. "You're family, after all. Well, not officially family *yet*."

The school was the same, but for me it was totally different. My ex-friends looked away or gave hesitant smiles in the hallway. I didn't smile back. Why bother?

I could hardly walk two steps without running into a Crip. They seemed to be everywhere. Eric and Black Chuck must have had something to do with it. They wanted to make sure I was protected.

At lunch, I sat with Eric and his blue crew. Despite their thuggish reputation, they were really warm and friendly. There was:

Rolo—whose name was Dexter, then became Rolo Dex, then just Rolo.

French—a right-off-the-boat Haitian.

Snoopy—not to be mistaken for another more senior member of the FJC called Snoop.

And Hex—whose mama cursed him every day.

As for girls, I met:

Apple Jax—aka Jackie.

Sly—aka Celine.

Jazz—aka Jasmine.

And of course, Sarah and Nessa.

Sitting with the Crips was like sitting with any other group in the caf, except that they wore a lot of blue and everybody was careful not to bump their table.

What did I expect—that they'd only talk about heinous ways to maim and humiliate Bloods? They were just regular people who talked about sports, parties, and love triangles. Maybe, without realizing it, Marie's constant Crip-bashing had gotten to me. They were nothing like the Blood-thirsty vampires she'd described.

Some Crips were obvious, rocking their colors in the hallways. But others dressed like everybody else, not wanting to flaunt gang gear in the faces of other gangbangers—or teachers and deans.

"We call them Sleepers," Nessa explained as she picked over her food. "They don't show themselves in school, but we call on them when we need them. Teachers usually think they're angels. Sleepers get stuff done, son."

Eric walked me to my dance class, giving me a kiss before I went in. His lips were cool from his soda, and soft.

"I'll be right outside the change room ten minutes before the end of your class. If I hear trouble, I'm coming in."

"There won't be trouble."

I walked into dance class, and Ms. Russo approached me. "It's good to have you back, Julia. Are you all right? You still look a bit banged up."

"I'm okay, thanks."

But as I went to sit down on the gym floor and started stretching, I wondered if I really was okay. I felt eyes on me—sympathetic eyes, curious eyes, hateful eyes.

Bitches Toneya and Lisa were watching me.

I looked at them.

You want to mess with me? my eyes dared them.

You're going down, their eyes said.

Ms. Russo was watching us. She cleared her throat loudly.

I *so* wanted to beat the shit out of them for what they'd done to me. But from what I'd heard, they'd already had the snot kicked out of them last week. They were lucky compared to Marie. Rumor had it she got cut pretty bad and would be out of school for a while.

There wasn't one part of me that felt sorry.

DECISION

So I had a decision to make.

Rain fogged up the bus windows, but I wasn't going to miss my stop. I knew where I was going: three lights and a right turn to go. I didn't know if it was the damp seats or the guy in front of me that smelled like mold, but it made me want to gag. I always got bus sick when it's rainy out, I don't know why.

The Crips. Sometimes I felt like I was a part of them already. I sat with them at lunch, chilled with them after school. But then they'd go off to a meeting or a party, and I was on the outside again.

I wasn't a Crip, and the girls wouldn't let me forget it. They wanted me to join the family.

If I didn't join, my days of hanging around with the Crips were numbered. I didn't know how long I'd have their friendship—and protection—if I didn't commit to them. Sure, they were putting up with me out of props for Eric and Black Chuck, but how long would that last?

The girls tried to sway me with promises of endless parties, but I wasn't going to join just so I could party with them. Sure, it would be cool to go to the exclusive parties Eric and Black Chuck talked about, but it wasn't the biggest reason to join.

If I joined, it would make the rest of my high school days a helluva lot easier. I wouldn't have to worry about people coming after me, since I would have the protection of the toughest kids around. I could walk with my head up. No fear.

Was it worth selling my soul to feel safe?

But I wouldn't be selling my soul. I knew that now. If I joined, I wouldn't have to participate in every single thing the gang was up to. The girls made me realize that gang members still had choices of their own and didn't have to get involved in every beef, every hustle, every bit of daily drama, just like they didn't have to go to every meeting or every party. I could be Crip, and what that meant would be up to me.

Still, I hesitated.

I hesitated because of the exit clause.

There wasn't one.

Once you're in, you're in. The girls made no secret of that.

The only official way out is to get jumped out. The last person who got jumped out got himself a broken jaw and a C carved into his back with a razor blade.

If I was going to join, I had to commit to it—at least till I was done with high school. After that, the girls said, I could move on, like if I wanted to go off to college. I'd always have friends when I came back to Brooklyn, though. I'd be Crip alumni.

I liked the idea of having friends to come back to. Friends who would always be there and who wouldn't walk away if things got complicated.

Yeah, I'd made my decision. I pulled the cord to get off the bus.

$CRAP

I rang the doorbell of a Flatbush Avenue townhouse.

Black Chuck answered the door. His eyes bugged out.

"What you doing here? We got a meeting."

"Then you answered your own question. I want to join, Chuck."

"*What?* Look, Ju, let's talk about this tomorrow."

He actually tried to close the door in my face. I blocked it with my arm.

"I'm serious. I want to ask Scrap what it takes to join."

"Why?"

"Do you have to ask why?"

A voice yelled from the kitchen, "*Who dat?*"

"Julia!" I called back, trying to get past him.

Black Chuck stopped me with his body. His eyes were inches from mine. "I asked why."

"Because I need you guys. I've got nobody else."

He let me pass. Scrap was in the kitchen drinking beer, a curvy twenty-something on his lap.

"Julia!" He swatted the girl's ass, then got up and hugged me real close. He didn't ask what I was doing there. I guess he knew. He looked me over and smiled, his grill silver and gold.

"*Julia?*" Eric had come up from the basement, spliff in hand. "What are you doing here?"

"Ain't it clear?" Scrap said. "Go back downstairs. We about to start the meeting."

Eric shot me a confused look, then went downstairs. The rest of us followed him.

I hadn't been in this basement for years. It had changed a lot. Torn-up couches and a small, crackly TV had been replaced with sleek leather couches and a huge plasma screen. A pool table was set up, and there was a marble bar in the corner stacked with liquor.

There were about twenty people in the room. Nessa and Jazz were there, big smiles on their faces. I squeezed onto the couch between Eric and Rolo. Eric didn't look at me.

He was pissed off. But why? I was going to be with him

one hundred percent now. We could share everything.

Maybe he was just upset that I'd taken him by surprise. Well, *he* didn't consult me when he'd joined the FJC. He, of all people, should understand that I had to make this decision myself.

Scrap stood up and everybody went quiet. "As you can see, we got ourselves a WB."

A wannabe member.

Me.

Everybody looked at me. I had the sudden, unexplicable urge to run.

What was I doing?

"Some of you know Julia, some don't," Scrap said. "Let's give her props for showing up."

To my surprise, people leaned over and pounded palms with me, smiled at me, kissed my cheeks. I felt myself relax.

Scrap said, "You see, Julia, we can't really have the meeting with a WB here, but we can talk about you joining. Brother Chuck, why don't you say something about Julia?"

Black Chuck was sitting on the arm of a chair. "Julia is a mad good friend, and mad loyal."

He sounded reluctant, but in the end, he'd supported my membership.

Thank you, Chuck. I smiled at him.

Somebody said, "She's smart at school. Teachers like her. We can always use low-key peeps like that." I turned my head. Holy shit—it was George Vaughn talking, Honors student and Student Council member! I'd never seen him with the Crips.

George winked at me.

He was a Sleeper.

I'd had no idea.

Scrap said, "Eric?"

"They don't come any better than Julia." Eric looked at me, his eyes unreadable.

Scrap turned my way. "The way I see it, you been almost-Crip for years now. But you gotta do two things to get in. One is to memorize our codes and pass a test. Chuck or Eric will help you with that later. The other is to choose a member to induct you."

I'd heard about induction, aka getting *jumped in*. This was the part where I let somebody kick my ass around. I was surprised that I'd actually be able to choose who would do it.

Rolo said, "I bet she never had that cherry popped, yo!"

What was he talking about? I looked around for an explanation.

The Crips laughed.

"You gotta fuck a Crip, Julia," Scrap said. "That's how we induct the ladies."

I froze. The girls never warned me about this!

"Chill, Julia," Scrap said, grinning. "You can choose who, but it can't be somebody you fucked before. I recommend my OG ass."

"I choose Eric," I said.

Everybody scoffed.

"Yeah, right!"

"Not fair!"

"Fucking her man is no induction!"

I felt my heart pounding in my throat. This could not be happening.

Run. I still had a chance to run.

"We haven't fucked yet," Eric said. "It's true."

"Come on, Scrap," Black Chuck said. "We can't prove they did it or not. Let her choose Eric."

"Yeah, let her have her man." It was Jazz.

Eric stared at Scrap. "My girl ain't gonna fuck anybody else."

"A'ight, a'ight," Scrap said. "It'll be Eric. Go upstairs now. Eric, I'll catch you up on the meeting later."

Eric grabbed my hand and we went upstairs to the kitchen, where he put his arms around me and hugged me so tight I could hardly breathe.

"You shouldn't have come here," he said against my hair. "It was a big mistake."

I pulled out of his arms. "If you can be a part of this, why can't I?"

"You don't belong here and you know it."

"News flash, Eric. I don't belong anywhere anymore. My friends ditched me. The RLB still wants to kick my ass. I *need* to be a Crip now."

"Fine." He grabbed my hand and practically yanked me up the stairs to the first bedroom on the right. "This is the induction room. Is *this* what you want?"

The room was bare except for an old dresser and a mattress with a couple of rumpled sheets on it.

"They've got a room especially for this?" I asked.

"Used to be their mom's bedroom." Eric closed the door behind us.

I sat down on the bed and started to cry. "I can't do it this way. . . ."

He put an arm around me. "I know, Julia. I was just making a point. I wouldn't do it with you here if you begged me. This room is disgusting."

I couldn't stop crying.

"Shhh . . . it's okay. We'll say we did it. We'll mess up each other's hair and shit. Got me?"

"I got you."

PREP

"When the sky is gray . . ."

". . . it's Crip day," I finished.

Black Chuck had appointed himself my Crip tutor. We sat in the A-raab place, our burgers and fries finished ages ago.

"You're doing good, Ju. Here's another one. What have you got in the fridge?"

"Blueberries and milk."

"Good. Summer is Blood or Crip time?"

"Summer is Blood season, winter is Crip season."

"What would I find in your closet?"

"A witch holding a glass of milk."

"Good. What color is your blood?"

"It's blue, but when it hits oxygen it turns red."

"No wonder you do so good in school, you got a great memory. I'll tell Scrap you're ready for the test anytime."

"I hope you're right."

THIS IS ONLY A TEST

The test took place in Black Chuck's kitchen. Scrap was smoking weed. He offered me some. I took a drag, but couldn't help coughing it out.

"Ready?" Smoke streamed from his nostrils.

I nodded.

He asked question after question. I aced them all. But then he asked, "Who started the Crips?"

"Tookie Williams." Thank God I'd seen the movie *Redemption*.

"Right, Stan Tookie Williams. Who started it with him?"

Shit! I didn't know this.

"Well?"

"I didn't know I had to study that."

"The answer is Raymond Lee Washington. Died in seventy-nine."

I wrung my hands. Did this mean I failed?

I *had* to pass.

If I didn't become a Crip I'd be on the outside.

Forever.

"I'll give you half points. Now, I'd like you to write the word *blood* on this paper." He slid a paper and pen in front of me.

What, he didn't think I could spell?

As I slowly wrote the word, I tried to figure out what he was getting at.

B . . . L . . . O . . . O . . . D . . .

My pen stopped on the last letter. The word needed something more, I could feel it.

Then it hit me.

Whenever Black Chuck wrote his name, he crossed out the B. I guess B symbolized Bloods and had to have a line through it.

I crossed out the B. Scrap clapped. "You passed, Julia! Welcome."

He took me to the basement where the others were waiting. They presented me with a handbook and flag.

Everybody clapped and hugged me and kissed me.

"She needs a new name," somebody said.

"I already thought of one," Scrap said. "We gonna call her Innocent. Don't she just look so innocent?"

Everybody agreed.

JOINED

I joined.
Staying out didn't work
Got me Jumped
Got me Fucked
Now I feel safe
They got my back because
I joined.
No Fear
Like before
My Colors, an ID badge
Like a family coat of arms
Like a welcome mat
For friends
Like a slamming door
For Bloods.

Qdancediva: i heard its official

PoeticJustiss: yea

Qdancediva: did u have to do some grimey stuff to get in?

PoeticJustiss: u know me. i dont do anythin i dont wanna do

Qdancediva: its hard to believe who ur hangin out with now. its weird

PoeticJustiss: wud it be better if i didnt have ANY friends?

Qdancediva: u know i dont mean that. i hope u werent upset i didnt talk to u in the caf today

PoeticJustiss: who cares? i was busy anyway

Qdancediva: i meant to IM u sooner but i got caught up with homework. if i keep my grades up i might take some ap classes next semester

PoeticJustiss: thats cool

Qdancediva: maybe u could too

PoeticJustiss: i still havent caught up on all the work i missed. im not gonna get over 90% in anythin except maybe dance

Qdancediva: can u believe vickys gonna fail dance? she has it last period and she cuts. i dunno what shes thinkin

PoeticJustiss: i dont wanna hear about vicky or any of the

girls ok? they dont exist to me anymore.
their choice not mine

Qdancediva: sorry. i hope u know were still gonna be
friends no matter what

PoeticJustiss: yea

ᴍEMBERSHIP PRIVILEGES

Sitting in American History class a week later, I couldn't believe how much my life had changed.

I glanced down at my blue fingernails.

Blue shoelaces.

Blue book bag, with the blue flag dangling from it.

I wasn't a sleeper. I was the real deal. I wanted people to know I was Crip.

It made the haters stay away.

It made people watch what they said around me.

And there was freedom in that.

It brought me a new group of girlfriends — Sarah, Nessa, Apple Jax, Sly, and Jazz — who treated me like one of their own. Yeah, they were a loud, fast, potty-mouthed bunch, but they were real and I loved them. If they had a problem with you, they'd tell you instead of tiptoeing around it. I respected that.

The sweetest part of joining the gang?

It brought Eric and me closer.

True, he still wasn't cool with the fact that I'd joined. He kept saying that he felt guilty—like he'd corrupted me or something. But he'd get over that eventually.

"You were a good girl before I met you, Divine," he told me last night on the phone.

"Yeah, I was good, and it got me jumped. At least now we've got people to stand up for us."

He'd come around. It wasn't like he ever suggested I try to get out of the gang. We both knew it didn't work that way.

The bell rang ending the class. I turned to Eric. "I'll meet you outside in a sec. I need to talk to Ms. Ivey."

I went to the front of the class, waiting for some kid to finish talking to her before I had my turn.

"Am I all caught up?" I asked.

"You're caught up." She didn't seem like she was in a very good mood.

"Is my grade going to stay the same this marking period?"

"The calculator will tell, Julia." She looked at me. "You have some new friends, I've noticed."

"Yeah, well, the old ones didn't stick around."

"I see. Would you tell them not to wave at you while you're in class? It distracts your classmates."

"Oh, sorry."

"Better get going. Your boyfriend is waiting for you."

"See you tomorrow," I said, backing away.

She didn't like me anymore, I could feel it.

What had I ever done to her?

I guess she was like my other teachers—when my colors changed, she'd changed. I'd thought she might be different. I didn't know why.

Outside the classroom, Eric was talking on the phone. He finished up when he saw me.

"Who was that?"

"Scrap."

"Is there trouble?"

"'Course not."

We went up a flight of stairs toward my next class.

"So I'll meet you at the usual spot after school?" I said.

"I'm cutting out early today."

"But then you'll have to go to makeup lab. What's so important that you have to leave early?"

"Damn, you sound like my mom."

"I was just asking where you were going. Something wrong with that?"

"Kinda feels like you're checking up on me."

I blinked. "Are you serious?"

"Don't worry about it. I'll call you tonight, okay?" He kissed my cheek and headed back downstairs.

I stared after him, a sinking feeling in my stomach.

I got home around 4 p.m., throwing off my jacket and tossing my keys on the table. I curled up on the couch with chips and a glass of milk. Oprah was about people who were badly disfigured. I turned away. I felt shitty enough already.

Eric had bitched at me for the first time.

Was it stupid to ask where he was going? Isn't that what girlfriends do? Why did he say I acted like his mom?

I had the urge to call Q, but I knew I couldn't do that. Her mom would probably answer the phone, and God knew what she thought of me now.

Damn it, I still had friends, didn't I? My Crips were there for me. Maybe I should start spending more time at Black Chuck and Scrap's place. It was FJC Central, after all.

Getting off the couch, I decided to stop feeling sorry for myself and go find some company.

I caught a bus down Flatbush Avenue. A few minutes later, I rang the doorbell. At first there was no answer, but I could hear people inside. I rang again.

Finally, I heard somebody coming to the door. I had the feeling I was being looked at through the peephole.

The door opened a crack—the latch was on.

Scrap peered out, face sweaty, eyes glassy.

"What up, Innocent?"

"Um, I just wanted to see what you're all doing. Is Black Chuck here?"

"He ain't home."

"Eric?"

"Nah. We're kinda busy here. Catch you later?"

"Okay."

The door closed.

Maybe I really was a disease.

I walked down the front steps, nearly tripping over a beer bottle left on the shitty excuse for a lawn.

On the corner, I ran into Black Chuck.

"Ju! You been partying with the crew?"

"I just got sent away."

"Oh. Guess they wanted to keep you . . . innocent."

"Is Eric in there getting high?"

Black Chuck spread his hands. "Look, I ain't saying nothing."

I walked off and dialed Eric's cell. I got his voice mail. "I hear you're at Scrap's getting high with everybody. Should I thank you for not inviting me?"

Five minutes later I got a text message.

IM SORRY. DONT WANT U DOIN THIS. U R MY DIVINE

INNOCENT

"You're not like the other chicks in the gang," Eric told me that night on my couch. "They're getting high, like, every night. Today the shit was harder. I didn't think you'd want to be around."

"You're right about that."

"Good. Don't ever let them tempt you. They like to see the innocent ones get fucked up."

"What about my girls—they weren't there, were they?"

"Nah, they weren't invited."

"So how does it work—you guys test it out before you sell it?"

Eric's eyes narrowed. "I don't sell or use. You know that."

"I know. But the others do, right? I mean, the lieutenants?"

"Yeah. I guess it ain't hard to figure out."

"Not hard at all. Look, Eric, just be careful. You could get caught if there's a raid."

"I've been thinking about that too. I'll be careful. Next time I'll find a reason to stay away. Anyway, they don't keep that shit in the house most of the time—they were just trying a new cut."

"You didn't try anything?"

"I told you I don't use. I won't say I haven't tried a few things in the past, but not anymore. Today I just had a few beers."

"I can smell that."

"Do I need a mint?"

"It's okay. What did you try—in the past?"

"It doesn't matter. Whatever I did, I tried to do it safely."

"Do it safely—yeah, right."

"Getting preachy on me?"

"No . . ." I looked into his eyes. God, those eyes made my insides melt. "I don't care if I act like your mom, Eric. I only do it because I love you."

Total mistake!

"Sorry, it kinda slipped out." My face felt hot. "I'm not trying to freak you out."

He lifted my chin. "You're totally freaking me out, Julia. But it's okay, because I know what you mean."

He kissed me. God, was he kissing me.

I loved him. So much. More than I should.

But I didn't care. I only cared that he was kissing me, and his hands were all over me.

I tasted beer in his mouth, and I liked it. I tasted him deeper, and he tasted me.

He groaned.

I gasped at the feel of his hard body coming down on top of me.

His hips ground against mine.

He wanted me.

Badly.

Like I wanted him.

"You drive me crazy. . . ."

"Eric . . ."

"Julia . . ."

"Don't worry, I won't . . ."

"I know you won't, let's just have . . ."

". . . fun . . ."

He pulled up my shirt and started kissing my stomach. Heat licked through my body. I closed my eyes, loving the sensations. His hands found my breasts.

Wow.

Oh WOW.

I stopped thinking. I grabbed his shirt and pulled it out of his pants, ripping it over his head, messing up his hair.

His chest was gorgeous. Lean, light brown. Hard with muscle.

He kissed my lips, my cheeks, my neck. I grabbed his shoulders.

He had a tattoo in between his shoulder blades.

A five-pointed crown.

I'd have to ask him what it meant—later.

For now . . .

. . . some FUN . . .

DADDY DEAREST

"Haven't seen Q in a while," Dad commented without looking up from the Sunday paper.

I was passing through the kitchen on my way to the door. I stopped in my tracks. "Haven't seen *you* in a while either, Dad."

That got his attention. His head snapped up. "What does that mean?"

"Nothing. I'll see you later." I headed for the door.

"*Julia.*"

"What?"

"Did something happen with your friends?"

"They blew me off. It happens."

"So who are you with all the time then? Eric?"

"Who are *you* with, Dad?"

He looked surprised. "Whoever they are, they've given you a real attitude."

"Nobody gives you an attitude. You have it or you don't."

"Look, if you're upset about your friends, why don't you tell me about it?"

"I'm not upset about my friends. You ask questions when it's convenient for you. You act like a dad when you feel like it. The rest of the time you're out with your girl or your buddies like I don't exist."

His face paled. "Is that how you feel?"

"No. I'm making small talk."

"I thought you appreciated your independence."

"I . . ." God, I was stupid. I hadn't realized the outburst was inside me until it came out. Why did I bother?

"I'll cancel my plans with Gina today. We'll go out for dinner."

"Thanks, but I'm meeting friends. I've gotta go."

"Wait."

Dad came over and hugged me.

All I could think was:

He'll get sympathy from Gina when she hears of his daughter's bitch-fit. *Maybe she's got PMS,* she'll say. *Don't worry, Tony. Let's go to a show.*

And he'll forget the whole thing.

As usual.

BEING BLUE

Being Blue on the streets of Flatbush was like being part of a big, loud, dysfunctional family. The daddy was Scrap. He wore the pants in the gang. Nobody who didn't want to get beaten or cut messed with him.

The mama was Latoya, Scrap's live-in girlfriend. She was the sister of Prince, head of the Flatbush Sha-Tas, a well-known gang imported from Jamaica. The relationship meant a truce between the two gangs, and an alliance against local Bloods and the Haitian Mafia. Latoya took care of everybody: her three kids (the last two by Scrap), the lieutenants, and the younger gang members. She fed us, gave us booze and blunts, and fought off nosy relatives who crashed our parties. Most of all, she babied Scrap 24-7.

The senior gang members were Scrap's "lieutenants." They were usually full-time hustlers. With no education or jobs, the lieutenants' lives revolved around the gang, and they did whatever Scrap asked them to do—jacked cars, robbed places, pimped, pushed drugs. Lucky for me, they kept the lower members in the dark about that shit, especially the hard dealing. I figured they weren't trying to protect us; they were protecting themselves. And that was fine with me. I didn't want to end up in juvey because I was in the wrong place at the wrong time.

Scrap's lieutenants—Karl, Fathead, Clyde, Max, and Messiah—were the shadiest group I'd ever met. When I was younger, I called guys like them "corner thugs" because they hung around on street corners, catcalling girls and being a pain.

Black Chuck's friend Rolo, aka Dexter Watson, was a lieutenant-in-training. According to Eric, Scrap would probably initiate Rolo on his eighteenth birthday, a few months off. He was a good choice because he had all the makings of a corner thug—he never went to school, he hustled anything he could get his hands on, and he'd been in and out of juvey for years. That's what happens when you can never pass a Blood on the street without getting into a fight.

Our hangouts were record shops, lounges, diners, and street corners. Party Central was Black Chuck's place, where peeps chilled most nights, smoking weed and playing Xbox, drinking Hennessy or Bud, eating greasy Chinese or Jamaican food.

You could count on a party every Friday night, with dozens of FJC, twenty flavors of weed, BYOB, and dancing girls. The nasty stuff went on downstairs and upstairs—so I stuck to the kitchen and den.

I got along great with the Crip girls who went to my school. Too bad the neighborhood FJC girls didn't warm up to me much.

"It's 'cause you new," Nessa explained.

"It's 'cause you pretty," Sarah said.

But to me it really didn't matter. I had a group of girlfriends now, and that was all I needed.

My closest friend was Jazz, aka Jasmine Hughes. She was a junior at South Bay too, and she'd been in the gang since she was a freshman. Her big brother, Clyde, was one of Scrap's lieutenants.

Jasmine was light-skinned with freckles, and always talking about losing twenty pounds. She talked trash like the rest of them, but deep down, she was sweet and sensitive—a closet poet. She and Clyde were being raised by their grandma, because their mom was in prison down in Florida, and their dad was nowhere to be found.

It wasn't unusual in the gang.

Once, when I bitched about my dad, Eric said, "You got nothing to complain about. Most of the Crip kids don't even have a dad. Some don't even have a mom. They grow up with relatives too damn old to take care of them. Or who just don't give a shit. Or foster parents who do it for the money. But at least they got the Crips."

Eric was right. We had a family bigger than our own.

SURVIVAL OF THE FITTEST

I met Black Chuck and Eric at the bus stop at 7:37 a.m. Black Chuck was pumped. "This is gonna be sick!"

"How many eggs have we got?" Eric asked.

"Only three dozen. Went to four different stores last night and that's all I could find." Black Chuck looked at me. "Better put your hood up. You don't wanna get Nair in your pretty hair."

"That's an urban legend. Nobody really does that."

"You're wrong, Ju. It happened to my cousin last year. At close range. Had to shave his head."

I swallowed.

"This shit is tame compared to DT," Eric said. "Last night was the big night—we call it Devil's Night. Whole damn city gets trashed."

The normally crowded bus was dead. The only one I recognized from South Bay was Ivan Kurtsov, a stocky, glasses-wearing Honors student. He gave us a solemn nod as if to say, "Good luck."

"You worried?" Eric asked, his eyes teasing.

"Not really."

"I still don't know why you wanted to go to school. You said nobody shows up on Halloween."

"Right, and teachers give out mad bonus points. I need those points. You should go to your classes—I bet you could use the points, too."

"I would, but we're meeting some Crips on the roof. I'm guessing when we're done we'll be taking off in a hurry."

"Oh. So you won't be around to walk me back to the bus stop?"

He grinned and kissed my hair. "Call my cell. I'll come get you."

When we got off the bus, the guys put their caps on and tucked some eggs into their pockets just in case. I put up the hood of my old raincoat. Scanning the area, we didn't see anybody suspicious. I looked down Avenue X toward the school. It had the eerie look of a ghost town.

We crossed Nostrand and started down Avenue X. Ivan was

right behind us. I wasn't at all sure there was safety in numbers, but I wasn't going to tell him to stop walking with us.

Eric and Black Chuck were scanning nearby alleys and rooftops for threats, hands in their pockets. We picked up the pace as we passed in front of the South Bay projects, the part of the stretch where we were the most exposed. We'd decided earlier that we were safer on this side of the road than if we walked past the stores, where snipers could pop up anywhere.

We crossed the street at the last possible second. We were almost in front of the school now. Just a few yards to go before we came under the protection of the security guards. Adrenaline pumped through my blood. We were going to make it. Sure, they'd probably spotted us, but—

Smack. An egg hit me square in the back. We swung around to see a bunch of kids crouched between parked cars, pelting us with a stream of eggs.

I felt Eric's hand push me along. "Go!"

I broke into a run, felt an impact against my shoulder, against my book bag. Ivan grunted as the eggs hit him, covering his head with his hands and muttering curses.

Eric and Black Chuck weren't running with us. I glanced back to see them holding their position behind a parked car, firing back. Chuck had dropped his bag and they were digging into it for more ammo.

Ivan and I did a 90-degree turn onto the school grounds, past two security guards. Once I knew I was safe, I stopped and looked back.

Eric and Black Chuck might be outnumbered, but they were stronger and had better aim than their attackers, who were probably freshmen. Two of the kids had already run off and the others were wearing down. Suddenly Eric and Black Chuck burst out from behind the car and ran straight for them. The kids took off down an alley beside a convenience store, the guys right on their heels.

I waited a few minutes for them to come back. When they did, they were out of breath but smiling.

"Hope you didn't hurt them too bad," I said.

Black Chuck grinned. "Let's just say they got their protein for the day."

Eric slapped him five. "Bodybuilder's cocktail, eh?"

We all laughed.

"Heading up to the roof now?" I asked.

"For all the good it'll do," Black Chuck said, shaking his head. "Wasted all our ammo on those little shits."

FUN, CRIP-STYLE

It was almost midnight. People gathered in the fenced-in yard of a local private school. Eric, sweetie that he was, used his switchblade to jerk open the locked gate so I wouldn't have to climb over the fence and tear my jeans.

A bunch of people dangled from the jungle gym. Eric grabbed a swing and pulled me onto his lap.

"It's brick out here," I said.

He opened his jacket and pulled me close.

I snuggled into his chest. "Are you gonna tell me what this thing is about?"

"Scrap organized it. Doesn't that tell you something?"

"We're going to see a fight?"

"You'll see."

"Hey, guys!" Jazz came up behind our swing and gave us a push. "What up?"

I hung on to Eric as we swung back. "Nothing. I have no idea what I'm doing here."

Jazz shot Eric a look. "You think this is Innocent's sorta thing?"

He shrugged. "She's part of us. She should know what we do."

A weird kind of excitement twisted my gut.

Five minutes after midnight, Scrap pulled up in his vintage Caddy. Latoya was with him. Black Chuck, Rolo, and Clyde jumped out of the back.

"Yo, everybody get into position!" Scrap shouted.

Crips jumped off the jungle gym into the sand. Eric lifted me off his lap and put me down. "Remember one thing, Divine. Whatever happens, don't get involved."

I frowned. "Whatever that means."

Everybody was forming a circle. We slid in beside Jazz.

Scrap went into the middle, doing a little dance and ending it with a spin. "How you doing?"

We shouted back.

"You hyped?"

"*Yeahhh!*"

"Good—tonight's gonna be off the hook! We got lots of new fighters. This first competition's gonna crack you up—meet Moe the Hobo and Slow Stan!"

Two grizzled homeless men stumbled into the circle.

I elbowed Eric. "What the hell is this?"

"Bum fight."

"What?"

"You heard me. Chill, nobody's gonna die."

"People are betting on this?"

"Yeah. Do you want to? I think Moe's gonna whoop Stan's ass."

"That's disgusting!"

The fight started. Moe slapped Stan, who touched his cheek like he didn't know what was going on. "You b-b-bastard!" Stan smacked back, and then they were grappling, pulling each other's hair, punching each other.

At one point, Rolo crept up behind them and pushed them both to the ground. Everybody cheered.

I watched in sick fascination. I wanted it to be over already, and yet I couldn't look away—until Moe had Stan pinned and started pounding his face.

"Stop it!" I screamed at Eric.

"Scrap will stop it."

And he did, seconds later. Scrap helped Moe off the ground, awarded him fifty bucks and a huge bottle of Absolut. Moe stumbled off.

Stan was having some trouble getting up. His beard was matted with blood. Nobody wanted to get near him. Eventually he got up by himself, took a towel from Latoya and his twenty bucks for participating, and walked off to the sound of mocking cheers.

"My stomach is sick," I said to Eric. "Are they all going to be like that?"

"No, that's the only bum fight tonight."

From Scrap's ride, Sean Paul pumped. Some of us started grooving. I wished I could forget what I'd just seen. Eric grooved behind me. Damn, he was good at distracting me.

I stopped moving when I saw the next fighters in flashy red robes.

They looked about twelve years old.

Scrap danced into the middle of the circle and then—his trademark spin. "The next fight is between two of the baddest motherfuckas in Brooklyn. Our boy gladiators: Peace and Feather."

Eric said, "Gladiator tradition. Gotta have pussy names."

"You know this is fucked up, right?"

"We're training the next generation."

"That doesn't make it any less fucked up."

The kids fought fast and vicious like two mini Mike Tysons on speed. I could hardly follow what was happening, but at some point Peace took control. He fought like a little demon, smashing a fist into his opponent's ribs, and another and another, hustling him out of the circle.

"Whoa, whoa, whoa!" Scrap grabbed the two kids by the backs of their necks. "I think we got a winner—young Peace, Marlon Jones!"

The kid pranced around in a victory dance, not caring that blood was pouring from his nose. The other kid cursed and stamped his foot, vowing revenge.

"I don't even wanna know what's next," I said. "I've seen enough. Can we go now?"

"Soon." Eric took his jacket off, handing it to me.

"Eric? It's fucking November."

"I know."

He started bouncing on his feet, throwing a couple of practice punches.

"Please tell me this isn't what it looks like."

Another two quick air punches. "You want respect—you have to earn it."

"Oh God. Who are you going to fight?"

"We'll see."

With the crowd cheering, Eric joined Scrap in the middle of the circle.

Scrap shouted, "My boy, Eric, volunteered to step up. And he says to me, serve him up anything! Eric, you gonna be a lieutenant one day, no doubt. So here's your competition." Scrap walked out of the circle, whipped his shirt off, and stalked right back in.

Holy shit!

Scrap flexed his muscles for the crowd to see. FJC was tattooed in gothic script across his pecs. His nipples had tiny metal bars through them.

Eric was hard-bodied too. He wore a black tank that hugged his muscles and showed off his diesel shoulders and arms. But I couldn't revel in his gorgeousness—not when his life was on the line.

Jazz touched my arm. "You're shaking! It'll be okay. Scrap likes him."

"Scrap likes himself more. What if he hurts him?"

"He'll be all right."

"He better, or I'm going after Scrap myself."

Jazz laughed. "You're so cute, Innocent."

But I wasn't kidding.

I watched, my heart in my throat, as they bounced on their toes. Scrap kept faking him out, tempting Eric to take the first swing, but Eric didn't take the bait. He waited until Scrap got frustrated and rushed him. Eric blocked Scrap's right hook, landing his own punch in Scrap's side. Scrap jumped back like it didn't even wind him.

What if Scrap is high? What if he can't feel pain?

Eric lunged forward with two quick jabs—one at Scrap's head, the other at his gut. Scrap blocked both jabs, coming back with a vicious uppercut—which Eric dodged, thank God. Determined to land a punch, Scrap kept swinging, battering Eric's forearms until he finally hit Eric's stomach. Eric stumbled back a little, but shot right back, pummeling a left-right combo into Scrap's tattooed chest.

The crowd went crazy.

Eric was unbelievable. I had no idea he could fight like that!

It turned me on.

Everybody started cheering for Eric. Scrap sucked his teeth, looking like he was going to lose it. Then he came at Eric fast and hard. He broke through Eric's block and clipped his jaw, then smashed his fist into Eric's gut. I cringed.

The crowd egged Scrap on in his counterattack. I waited for Eric to bounce back, but he stayed defensive.

"Get him, Eric! Snuff him!" I shouted. But Eric wasn't hitting back. I saw one of his forearms drop, leaving his face exposed to a devastating right hook. Eric fell to the ground.

"Eric!" I ran over to him, helping him sit up. "Oh my God, are you okay?"

"Uh . . . yeah." Blood dribbled down the side of his face from a cut above his eye. "That was kinda fun."

"Are you kidding me?"

The crowd cheered for its leader. Scrap danced around, flexing his sweat-slicked muscles. When he was through posing, he gave Eric a hand, helping him to his feet. He asked the crowd, "How did y'all think my boy did?"

They cheered.

Scrap slapped his back. "You did good, Eric. From now on, you can be my protégé."

Eric wiped the blood out of his eye, and grinned.

"You're crazy," I said as we walked home. "Why did you volunteer to fight?"

"Maybe I had something to prove."

"Like what, that you're insane?"

"That I can hold my own."

"But it was so unfair. Scrap tricked you into fighting him!"

"Nah, I knew I'd be fighting him. It was my idea. Thing is, Scrap didn't want everybody to know that I'd fight him willingly. He likes people to think he's some fucking legend that we're all too scared to mess with. So he pretended to take me by surprise."

"Where'd you get the balls to challenge him?"

"I've dealt with much worse. And back then, they were really trying to kill me."

"That scares me, Eric."

"Why? You saw that I can defend myself."

"Yeah, but . . . Why are you laughing?"

"You're so cute when you're worried, Divine." He hugged me to his side. "I think you care more about me than my mom ever did."

"I'm sure she'd freak out if she saw you fight Scrap."

"You don't know my mom. If I ever came home saying I got hit, she'd ask me one thing: Did you beat the shit out of whoever did this to you? I always did, of course."

"That's some twisted shit."

"She did me a favor. Toughened me up."

"She'd be proud tonight, then. You really gave Scrap a run for his money. Better than anyone else in the gang could have. Next time you'll flatten him."

"No way. I can't fight Scrap and win. It would ruin his rep."

"What? Are you saying you threw the fight?"

"You didn't hear it from me, Divine."

"Well, did you or didn't you?"

"I thought I made that pretty clear."

"You actually threw the fight because you didn't want to embarrass Scrap?"

"I can't think of a better reason."

"C'mon, Eric, you really could've beaten him?"

"Yeah. He fights messy. He's strong, but he's got no training."

"And you do?"

"Maybe."

Qdancediva:	i thought u should know marie is coming back to school tomorrow
PoeticJustiss:	what does that have to do with me?
	oh i get it. its a warning
Qdancediva:	its not a warning i just dont want u to be

	taken by surprise
PoeticJustiss:	maybe thats what she wants. be careful q
	she might call u a snitch if she finds out
	ur warning me
Qdancediva:	would u tell her?
PoeticJustiss:	of course not. anyway its probably a
	good thing u told me ill watch my back
Qdancediva:	have u thought about changing schools?
PoeticJustiss:	no way thats exactly wat the bitches want.
	not gonna happen
Qdancediva:	i dont blame u. uv always been strong.
	i dont know where u get it from
PoeticJustiss:	sometimes u dont have a choice

RAZOR BLADE

Not only was Marie back at school, she was looking for me.

It didn't matter that I wasn't the one who cut her. In her mind, I was still the snitch.

All morning people whispered that there was going to be a fight. Screw them. Even though Marie was looking for me, I wasn't going to go looking for her.

A note was dropped on my desk.

> Marie wants to meet you in the front
> entrance at 11:30.
> Don't be a Crab Punk.
> Show your face!

I crumpled the note, then looked up. Several people were watching me.

Marie had publicized the challenge, no doubt.

I guess she had something to prove.

If she wanted to fight, why choose the front entrance? There were always security guards nearby.

Maybe that was the point. Maybe she didn't want to fight.

Yeah, right.

Maybe whatever she pulled on me, she wanted it to be real public.

Whatever she was planning, I didn't have a choice but to go.

But I wasn't going alone.

The front entrance was crowded with kids changing classes. Security guards blew their whistles and tried to direct them toward the lunchroom or their classes. As usual, nobody listened.

I spotted Marie and five Bitches right away, standing in front of the trophy showcases. Me and my crew stopped a few yards away, to the left of the cafeteria doors.

I made a "come here" sign to Marie. We both walked forward, meeting in front of the cafeteria doors. As I got closer, I realized that Marie looked different. She'd put on weight in the time she'd been laid up, and she had a two-inch scar on her cheek. Under different circumstances, I might've felt sorry for her.

"What do you want?" I asked her, straight up. "Is this your idea of a good place to fight?"

Marie looked me dead in the eye. "I wanted to show you something."

My pulse pounded. I was ready for her to whip out a blade anytime.

She thrust out her arm and pulled up the sleeve of her shirt.

She had a new tattoo, freshly done and covered with Vasoline.

It was the word *crab* upside down.

It was supposed to provoke me. To make me lose it and punch her. Give her an excuse to hit me back. Get me suspended in front of a whole bunch of people.

I didn't react the way she expected. I went, "Ugh! You scarred yourself for life!"

"Don't you see what it says?"

"Yeah. So what?"

"So what are you gonna do about it, Crab?"

I took a step closer, adrenaline pumping through my blood. "You want me to snuff you so that you can snuff me back. Cut my face with the spike on your name ring. Don't think I didn't see it, Marie. I've been hit by that ring before."

She swallowed. I realized that she was just as nervous as I was.

But I also knew she wouldn't walk away without a fight. She needed revenge for getting cut.

"You already fucked me up, Marie. And you got fucked up in return. I never asked for you to be cut, but I can't say I was sorry when I heard. I want to end this right now. If the only way you can save face is to fight, that's fine with me. But take off your fucking ring."

"You don't make the rules."

"If you try to cut me, you'll get it right back."

"You? Carrying a blade? Don't you get your Crab friends to do that for you?"

I ignored that. "Put your ring in your pocket, Marie. And I'll drop my razor blade."

She looked down at my hand, which was dug into my pocket. The last thing she wanted to do was negotiate with me, but more than that, she didn't want to get slashed again.

"Deal."

I took my hand out of my pocket, leaving behind the razor blade Nessa had given me. Marie lifted her hand out of her pocket without the ring. And then she jumped at me, grabbing for my hair.

I'd greased it back tight in preparation for this. All she could snag was the front of my shirt.

I got in a few punches. So did she. But then security was on top of us, dragging us away from each other.

They hustled us into the dean's office, where we both got suspended.

Or as most of us called it:

A three-day vacation.

LIVING IN THE GRAY

Dad didn't freak out when I told him about the suspension. Maybe that's because I told him I'd kicked the ass of the girl who beat me up. I think he was proud.

He didn't even bitch when he had to take off work for the suspension hearing.

I didn't care too much either. It just sucked that my teachers—like Ms. Ivey—were going to hear about it. She'd be thinking that I'd changed so much since joining a gang.

But she really didn't know anything about me.

Ivey was from the suburbs. She saw the world in black and white. Good and evil. Right and wrong. She didn't get gray.

I *lived* in gray.

Just because I was in a gang didn't mean I was screwed up or throwing my life away. I decided to get the highest mark in American History possible, just to show her.

I was going to use my suspension days to get started on my term project. I'd already picked my topic:

THE HISTORY OF GANGS IN AMERICA.

Last week I'd handed in my project proposal, and she'd passed it back with the comment: *Sounds fascinating. Make sure to include kids' reasons for joining gangs, typical gang activities, and the destinations of gang members.*

Destinations?

I knew what she was getting at.

Jail.

Rehab.

Cemetery.

Well, this gangbanger had every intention of going to college, no matter what the stats said.

I hopped the 2 train to Eastern Parkway and went to the main branch of the Brooklyn Public Library. On the computer, I looked up gangs.

Three hundred and ninety-six titles.

I went through the first few, wrote down some call numbers, and went in search of the books. I was going to take out as many books as I could carry. Ms. Ivey would be stunned when she saw all my research.

I put the books down on one of the long wooden tables in the main study room. The place was packed, mostly with people in their twenties and thirties who looked like they'd gone back to school.

I took some notes from Tookie Williams's autobiography, especially the part about why he started the Crips.

As I looked through the books, I was amazed at how many gangs there were. I hadn't even heard of most of them.

I wrote in my notebook: *Is it human nature to want to be part of a gang or some kind of club?*

Maybe my essay would argue that it was. Ms. Ivey was going to love that!

One of the books had a whole section with glossy pictures of gang clothing, symbols, graffiti, etc. The tattoos were fascinating. Some people covered their whole bodies with gang symbols. The letters were often in gothic script like Scrap's. There were Biker tattoos, White Supremacist tattoos, Blood tattoos, Crip tattoos, Latin Gang tattoos, Asian Gang tattoos. . . .

And then I stopped flipping pages and stared at one photo.

It was a five-pointed crown.

I'd seen that tattoo before.

On Eric.

The five-pointed crown, it said, was a popular symbol of the Latin Kings.

I blinked. It made no sense that he would choose the tattoo of a rival gang. Could he have gotten the tattoo without knowing what it meant?

Or was it possible that Eric used to be a Latin King?

"Eric?"

"Hey, Divine." Street noise in the background. "Can I call you back?"

"Sure. Just call back soon."

"Everything okay?"

"I hope so."

"What do you mean?"

"I have a question to ask you. It's about your tattoo."

Horns beeping, people talking, trucks going by.

"What about it?"

"It's the Latin Kings' symbol."

"I know. Stupid, huh?"

"You knew what it was?"

"Not when I got it. I'll stop by later and explain."

"Okay."

"See you later, Divine."

Eric buzzed at 10:44 p.m.

"Eric and I are going to Hal's for a snack," I told Dad.

"Isn't it kind of late for that?"

"He just got off work." I'd told Dad that Eric bussed tables at a restaurant in the city. He wouldn't have wanted me dating a guy without some kind of job. Truth was, Eric had been trying to find a job for a couple of weeks now, but no luck yet.

I met Eric when I got out of the elevator. He grabbed me and kissed me, then took my hand as we stepped into the night.

"Any leads on a job?"

He shrugged. "I handed out résumés at a few places in Park Slope. I'll wash dishes or bus tables, I don't care, as long as there's a chance I can move up."

"I hope you get a call soon."

"Me too."

"So . . . don't keep me in suspense. Tell me about that tattoo."

He laughed. "What's the matter? Tattoo got you freaked?"

"I don't know. Should I be?"

"No. It's a stupid story. Back in eighth grade, me and my buddies started our own gang and wanted to get tattoos. When we went to the tattoo place, one of them pointed out the five-pointed crown, said his brother had it. None of us knew any different."

"Were you guys pissed off when you found out?"

"*Were we?* Tattoos like this can get you killed. And people wonder why I never take my shirt off playing ball."

He opened the door for me as we went into Hal's. I inhaled the comforting smell of grease. The place was open until midnight, but right now it was empty except for a couple of guys eating at the counter.

The waitress came up as soon as we sat down. I ordered a hot chocolate and Eric ordered a Coke.

"Have you thought about getting it removed?"

"Of course. But I don't have that kind of bread."

"Are you going to get an FJC one?"

"Nah, I don't need a tattoo to show my allegiance. I got my colors and my flag for that. You get a tattoo, it's for life, and you know I won't be hanging with the Crips forever. It isn't part of my master plan."

I liked hearing him talk that way—of a future that didn't involve the Crips.

"Don't cut too many classes if you want to graduate in June," I said. "A lot of seniors get screwed that way."

"Trust me, Julia, I won't be messing up. I can't wait to leave high school behind and get on with my life."

Hopefully not leaving *me* behind too. "I hope we'll still see a lot of each other after you graduate. I mean, I know you'll be busy with cooking school and stuff . . ."

He looked me in the eye. "That is one thing I can promise you, Julia. I will never leave you behind."

THE PARTY, PART 2

The lights were low, the air thick with smoke. Fresh hip-hop tunes spun on the stereo system.

"I wonder what your mom would think if she came home and saw this," I said to Black Chuck between sips of Alizé.

"She'd say it was like old times, and tell me to roll her a spliff."

"Shouldn't she be back from rehab soon? She's been there for months, hasn't she?"

Black Chuck shrugged. "She don't keep us posted. She could be with her junkie friends in Hoboken, for all I know."

"Sorry."

"Don't matter."

"Do you ever get tired of having the party house? I mean,

some Fridays don't you ever want to chill by yourself?"

He raised an eyebrow, which was shaved in vertical lines. "Would it matter if I did?"

I got the picture.

I looked up and saw that I was being watched. Scrap winked at me, smiled his metallic smile. I guess he liked my sexy new outfit—the fake black leather pants and the tight black halter with a fat pink rose over my right breast. I'd picked out the outfit with the help of Jazz and Apple Jax on one of my days off (aka my suspension).

I'd worn it for Eric, of course. I knew he'd love it. Too bad he wasn't here yet to see it.

In the meantime, I obviously had Scrap's approval. Not that that was much of a compliment, since he had a rep for being a walking boner.

Nessa grabbed my hand. "C'mon, we dancing in the basement!"

I was up for that. "Chuck, you coming?"

"Later. We got pizza coming."

A bunch of people were dancing downstairs to Cam'ron's latest. There wasn't much room to dance between the couches, so people bumped and grinded, everybody getting hyped up.

As I danced, I thought of Q, and how we used to bust it out on the dance floor. I shoved the thought aside and focused on the people around me: Nessa, Jazz, Sly, Sarah, Apple Jax—all my girls were here. They'd stick by me, these girls. Not like my old friends.

K-RON came on. Nobody could put me in the dancing mood like him. I closed my eyes and moved to the music, then felt hands on my hips.

Eric!

I looked over my shoulder. It was Scrap.

I had no choice but to grind with him. Walking away would make him look bad, and you just didn't do that to Scrap. For his ego, I played along.

After a while, he moved on to the next girl, Apple Jax. Jazz went in front of him, making a Scrap sandwich. He seemed to be having a great time. I left the dance floor and ducked into the bathroom to call Eric.

I flicked the light on and was closing the door when Scrap pushed his way in and closed it behind him.

He took the cell phone from my hand and snapped it shut.

"Who you calling, baby?"

"Uh, Eric."

"What's wrong, you nervous? It's only me, Scrap. I known you since you was little."

"I have to go to the bathroom."

"No, you don't, honey. Don't be shy, now. Old Scrap's just looking for a little fun."

He put his hands on my shoulders, his pierced nipples jutting out of his shirt. "Eric wouldn't mind, if that's what you worried about."

"And Latoya?"

"Her pussy's all dried up. But yours is off the hook, honey. Eric said it himself."

He kissed me fiercely, drowning me in beer-breath and cologne. I pushed him back.

His eyes bulged. "Don't play me, Innocent. You always be smiling at me like you want me. Grinding with me on the dance floor. And now you playing hard to get?"

That got my back up. "I never led you on, Scrap. Why don't you back off?"

He slapped me.

"You a cock-block, Innocent." He walked out and slammed the door.

I locked it behind him, leaning against the door, my whole body shaking. Glancing in the mirror, I caught sight of the made-up face, the tear-filled eyes, the trembling chin.

Five minutes later, I'd pulled myself together enough to leave the bathroom and go upstairs. I grabbed a slice of pizza and sat down next to Black Chuck.

"You okay, Ju? You quiet."

"Cramps."

"Sorry. You want me to free up a bed so you can lie down?"

"That's okay."

When Eric showed up, I wanted to throw myself into his arms and tell him everything. But I couldn't trust how he'd react.

He'd probably confront Scrap.

Which is not something you did.

The whole gang would side with Scrap and fuck Eric up. I couldn't let that happen.

"She don't feel well," Black Chuck explained.

"You're pale, Julia," Eric said. "What's the problem?"

"Cramps. Could you walk me home?"

"Sure, come on."

I got my jacket and we went outside.

"Shit, it's cold," I said, stuffing my hands into my pockets.

"Are you gonna tell me what's wrong or what?"

"I said I had cramps."

"You suck at lying."

I guess I did.

I took a deep breath, choosing my words carefully. "It pisses me off the way Scrap is in control of everybody. He tells people what to do, he—"

"That's what gang heads do. That's normal."

"Maybe, but I don't have to like it. It's not just that he tells people what to do, it's the way he treats them. You should have seen him trying to get with half the girls at the party, right under Latoya's nose and with his babies upstairs!"

"He's an OG. That's what OGs do. You have to stop caring so much, Julia. You'll never be happy in the gang if you keep questioning things and bitching about how unfair it all is."

"But it *is* unfair. Scrap's got too much power, if you ask me. His lieutenants are like . . . sheep!"

"Maybe they like it that way."

"What do you mean? Why would anyone like being told what to do?"

"Maybe they hope to be head one day."

"When Scrap retires or dies?"

"When he goes to jail, probably."

"Is that how you see it? That Scrap's destined to go to jail?"

"Most of the lieutenants will do a few bids. That's the way it is."

"Doesn't that scare you?"

"Me? 'Course not. I'm not a pusher. I've seen too many friends in DT go down that way. The money's good for a little while, but it ain't worth it. Anyway, no matter what you think about Scrap and his lieutenants, you better keep your mouth shut. You say a bad word about Scrap and you're the hater of the month."

I knew I'd seriously pissed off Scrap. Would he send girls after me to teach me a lesson? But then, he'd have to admit that I rejected him—and he wouldn't risk the embarrassment, would he? I counted on that.

I noticed four Hispanic guys walk out of a housing project across the street.

"Maybe you should put away your flag," I whispered.

"Too late. They already saw it."

"Are they . . . ?"

"Cholos." Cholos was a rival gang. Meeting them this way would *not* be a good thing. They were coming toward us.

"I have pepper spray," I said quietly.

"If it's small enough to fit in your pocket, it won't work on four people." His hand tightened on mine. "If I tell you to run, run."

"If they want your cash, give it to them. Don't be a hero."

The guys walked up behind us. I tried to pick up the pace, but Eric held me back. "No point."

We turned around to confront them.

The oldest of the guys, probably twenty-five, gave a chip-toothed grin.

Shouldn't we be running by now?

The guy said something to Eric in Spanish. I heard the word "dinero"—money—and I assumed it was the Spanish equivalent of "run your pockets."

Eric didn't blink. He took out a blunt, lit it, and started smoking it right in front of them. He replied in Spanish, but the only word I caught was "Mexicans." The guys looked at one another like they didn't know what to make of what Eric was saying. That made five of us.

The guy wearing the white do-rag said something back.

Eric reached into his pocket, took out a few blunts and gave them to the guys. He used his lighter to fire them up. Then he pounded their palms, and we walked off.

When we got farther away, I gaped at him. "What just happened?"

"They were looking for an old-fashioned shakedown." Eric took a drag of his blunt and exhaled slowly. "But they were willing to compromise."

"Why'd you take the chance? We could've given them money!"

"I'd have preferred that—those spliffs were ten bucks a pop! But I figured this was a better way. It's showing them we can be cool with one another without running anybody's pockets. I'm in this hood all the time, you see. If I act like a punk once, they'll never leave me alone."

"But what if they wanted to fight you?"

"Then we'd fight." He put an arm around me. "You could watch from the sidelines, boo."

"Are you kidding me? Do you think I'd just watch?"

"Nah, you'd get in there with those fancy fingernails!"

"Glad you find this funny."

DAD TRIES

"Want to go out for dinner, bella?"

My eyes narrowed. Was this a setup of some kind? "Did Gina cancel?"

"No. I thought maybe you'd give your dad a couple hours of your time."

Talk about a one-eighty. Since when was he wanting time with me?

"Sure, if you're buying. I've been craving a cheeseburger deluxe."

"Great. We'll go to Jimmy's then."

Jimmy's was a huge diner on the corner of Flatbush and DeKalb Avenue. Its decor was loud and obnoxious, just like its customers. The tip from the last customer was still on our table when we sat down.

"I dare you to take that, Dad."

"You're crazy."

Dad had something on his mind—it was mad obvious—but he waited until after the waiter took our order before saying anything. "You're going out a lot more these days."

This was his way of being subtle, right? "Yeah. I'm having fun."

"Now don't get angry, but I'm wondering why you're not hanging around with that group of girls anymore."

"People drift apart, you know. It's not a big deal."

"That's not what you said before. You said they blew you off."

"Maybe I don't want to rehash the details, okay?"

"Fine. So who are you hanging around with then?"

"Eric and Black Chuck and some others."

"From your school?"

"Yeah."

"I had a lot of friends when I was your age too. Didn't hurt that I played sports. I haven't kept in touch with most of them over the years. They were never really a good influence on me. We were just drinking buddies, to tell you the truth."

Oh, I knew where this was going.

"So these kids you're spending time with, what do they do for fun?"

"Gangbang, hustle, pimp, drink, smoke, shoot up—the usual."

Dad burst out laughing.

I smiled. "I'm good, aren't I?"

He didn't know how good.

"Dad, what's this about? Are you worried I'm on drugs or something?"

"Of course not. I know you're not stupid. But you've been staying out late on school nights and I want to make sure you understand—I don't believe in curfews, but the second I hear you're slacking at school or cutting classes, I'll put you in lockdown."

Wow, Dad was laying down the law for the first time ever.

"I'll keep it under control, Dad. I didn't know you were worried."

"Tell me more about your new friends."

"What do you want to know?"

"Do these kids smoke up?"

I rolled my eyes. "This is so wack. I thought you trusted me."

"I do. I don't know if I can trust them."

The waiter came back with our food. I grabbed for the ketchup. Dad got it first, but gave it up. The food smelled delicious. I dug in.

After a couple of minutes, Dad said, "Don't be mad at me, Julia. I know you've had a rough time these past few weeks. I just want to make sure you're okay."

"I get it, Dad. You can relax. The concussion didn't screw up my brain."

Poor Dad. He could be annoying, but I could never really be mad at him for long. He was cute when he tried to be parental.

I took a few more bites of my burger. Dad had gone quiet, so I realized it was my turn. "How are things going with Gina? Sounds like things are going good."

"Yeah, she's a great girl."

"Ever think about getting married?"

He nearly choked on his food. "Are you serious?"

I shrugged. "Why not? You're with her all the time. That must mean something."

"Well, I like her a lot, but I can hardly see going to extremes like that. You know how it is."

I wasn't sure if I did.

JAZZ

It was a regular week until Jazz showed up at the door of Economics class with tears streaming down her cheeks.

Mr. Finklestein opened the door. She pointed at me, and he let me go talk to her.

"What happened, Jazz?"

She sniffed. "Let's go outside first. I don't wanna get taken to the holding room."

We went outside through a side door, jamming it with her book bag so we'd be able to get back in without going through security.

Jazz grabbed me, sobbing on my shoulder.

"Jazz, tell me what's going on!"

"I'm pregnant."

"What?"

"I'm so stupid. He—he was giving me all this attention."

"Who?"

"Scrap."

Oh no. Oh God.

"Scrap told me he'd liked me for a while but didn't know what to do about it because of Latoya."

"When was this?"

"A month ago."

"That bastard!"

"It's not his fault, Julia. He didn't force me."

"Why'd you do it?"

"Because I liked him. I thought he liked me. But he said to get rid of it." She was almost hyperventilating. "He didn't say that to Latoya! She's got two of his babies!"

"He's going to have to pay child support. Don't worry, Jazz, he's got money to help you out."

"That's what I said. I told him I wasn't gonna get rid of it, and he'd have to pay. Then he said he didn't even know if it was his! He said he didn't know how many guys I been fucking!"

"You'll prove it, Jazz. With DNA. Then you'll sue his ass for child support."

"I can't sue Scrap—he'd kick me out of the gang! He'd fuck me up, and Clyde too."

"Does Clyde know?"

"No. How can I tell him? He'll go after Scrap!"

I couldn't stand it. Scrap got away with everything because we were all too scared to stand up to him.

Not me. Not anymore.

"The doctor at the clinic says I need prenatal care, but I don't have insurance. Grandma's gonna kill me!"

"I'll get Scrap to give you some money. He's got plenty to spare."

"How are you gonna do that?"

"I don't know yet. I'll think of something."

I left school early and went right to his crib.

No answer.

Damn it.

I called Black Chuck's cell.

"Holla, honey."

"Chuck? Where are you?"

"On my way home. Where you at?"

"I'm standing outside your place. We need to talk."

"I'll be there in fifteen. Everything okay?"

"You'll see." I hung up. And waited.

When I saw Black Chuck coming around the corner, I ran up to him.

"What's the drama, Ju?"

"Scrap fucked up. And he's got to clean it up."

"Huh?"

"Remember at the party, when I said I wasn't feeling well? It was because Scrap tried to get me to sleep with him."

"C'mon, Ju, you can't take Scrap serious. He always playing."

"He followed me into the bathroom. When I told him no, he slapped me and called me a cock-block."

Black Chuck shook his head. "Aw, shit. I'm sorry."

Sorry? Why was he sorry?

Because he knew Scrap was like this. And he hadn't warned me.

"Don't be sorry, Chuck. It's not your fault. I'm only telling you now to give you background to the rest."

"The rest of what?"

"Scrap's been making the rounds. Last month he went after Jazz. She's pregnant."

"Holy shit. You sure?"

I nodded.

"Fuck!"

"Jazz knows Scrap won't be much of a baby daddy. But she needs money to go to the doctor while's she pregnant. I'm going to ask Scrap for the money. He should do right by Jazz and pay up. If he really doesn't think he's the daddy, he can pay for a DNA test once the baby's born. For now, she needs his help."

"Look, Ju, I'm glad you sticking up for Jazz and all, but I'll take it from here. I'll get the money from him."

"Are you sure?"

"You a bad bitch when you wanna be. I don't think he'd wanna hear what you have to say."

"Somebody's got to set him straight," I said. "Maybe after Jazz gets the money, we should tell Latoya. She's the only one who isn't scared of him."

"No way. You know what happens if she turns on him? Crip and Sha-Ta truce breaks down."

"We need to protect him because of the Sha-Ta?"

"You don't get it. They the ones keeping an eye on the Haitian Mafia for us. We dealing with as much as we can handle with the Bloods and the Latin gangs trying to close in. Nah, Ju, we need the Sha-Ta, and we need Latoya. She can't know he's been creeping on her."

"So what do we do about Scrap?"

Black Chuck sighed. "Maybe giving up the dough will teach him a lesson, or at least make him more careful about wrapping it up."

OLD FRIENDS

Qdancediva: its been a while how u been?

PoeticJustiss: all right u?

Qdancediva: ok. it sucked that u got suspended 4 fighting marie i hoped it wouldnt come to that but I know u had no choice. marie can be psycho

PoeticJustiss: its ur choice if u wanna hang with a psycho

Qdancediva: truth is i dont hang around with her as much these days. we got no beef though and i wanna keep it that way

PoeticJustiss: good luck with that

Qdancediva: the group sucks without you. sometimes i hang around with melisha just her n me.

vickys so immature

PoeticJustiss: shes takin after queen bitch marie

Qdancediva: ur right n u know what? vickys getting closer and closer to rlb these days. lisa martinez n toneya pierre even come to our girls nights

PoeticJustiss: holy shit u know what that means

Qdancediva: yea its only a matter of time b4 she joins rlb

PoeticJustiss: what would melisha do?

Qdancediva: she says she doesnt wanna join but that doesnt mean she wont

PoeticJustiss: shit. drama never seems to end

Qdancediva: i know what u mean. anyway i meant to tell u congrats on ur history project

PoeticJustiss: u heard about it?

Qdancediva: ivey said u got the highest mark in all three classes and shes mad stingy with marks

PoeticJustiss: the paper was on the history of gangs in america. she gave me 95%

Qdancediva: wow does that mean u might get into ap class next semester?

PoeticJustiss: im not interested. i dont need the extra work

	im too busy with other things
Qdancediva:	like what?
PoeticJustiss:	chilling writing eric
Qdancediva:	thats no surprise

BLOW

"Julia?" he croaked.

"Eric? Are you sick?" I said into the phone.

"Yeah. For once I got an excuse for not going to school. I think it's the flu. Everything hurts. My head. My throat. Even my damn skin hurts."

"Oh no! What about the game? You've been looking forward to it for ages!"

"Don't remind me. Why don't you use the tickets to take a friend?"

"You can't get your money back?"

"Nah."

"Maybe I'll take Jazz. She's been down lately. This could really pick her up."

"I was thinking of Black Chuck. He wilds out over the Giants. Unless you think Jazz is really into football."

"I guess you're right. I'll give Chuck a call. Then I'll stop by and pick up the tickets."

"Don't worry about that. Hex will drop the tickets off to you."

"Hex is taking care of you? That's sweet."

"Yeah, right. He's only here because I owe him money. Anyway, call Chuck. Hex will be there soon."

"All right. Hope you feel better."

"Me, too. Thanks, Divine."

I called Black Chuck.

"Holla, Chuck!"

"Holla back. What's cracking?"

"I got an extra ticket to the Giants game and wondered if you'd do me a favor and come with me."

"You bet your ass! When is it?"

"Tonight."

"Tonight! I can make it. Wait a minute, how'd you get the tickets?"

"Eric bought them. But he came down with the flu."

"That's wack. What time's the game?"

I laughed. Eric was right. Black Chuck did love football.

He got to my crib less than an hour later.

"Ran into Hex downstairs. He gave me the tickets." Black Chuck waved them like a winning lotto ticket.

"Don't be surprised when Eric hits you up for the hundred bucks he paid for it," I said.

Black Chuck's jaw dropped.

"I'm playing!"

"Shit, don't scare me like that! I'm mad dry these days."

"I know what you mean." I grabbed my jacket and scarf. "I'm ready. Let's dip."

We walked down Flatbush toward the Church Avenue subway. I felt something soft and wet brush my cheek. I realized it was snow.

Black Chuck zipped up his jacket. "Damn, I'm moving to Florida when I graduate."

"When's that gonna be?"

He glanced at me. "That's grease, Julia. I'm gonna get it together next semester, you'll see. I don't wanna be at South Bay when I'm twenty like Scrap was. He felt so old that he just stopped going."

"Did you talk to him about money for Jazz yet?"

"A little. But I gotta talk to him more."

"I know what that means."

"Chill, Ju. He'll come around. She don't need the money yet, right?"

"She'll need it soon."

"Don't worry. Black Chuck is on the case. How's Jazz anyway?"

I sighed. "Not good. Her grandma won't even speak to her, and she hasn't told her brother yet."

"Poor Jazz. She ain't gonna have it easy."

"Tell me about it."

When we got to the train station, we followed the signs to the 4/5 track and waited. Chuck was looking good in black and white. It hit me that he wasn't wearing his colors. He'd even taken the blue shoelaces out of his kicks.

Black Chuck was taking a night off.

I was glad.

The Game

The game was off the hook!

We nearly lost our voices from cheering the Giants and heckling the Eagles. We ate chili cheese dogs and hot pretzels and drank jumbo sodas and made fun of a group of fat white guys who were drunk enough to rip their shirts off in December.

I didn't get home until after eleven. I called Eric, but his phone was off.

I was brushing my teeth when the phone rang. Spitting out the toothpaste, I picked up. "Hello?"

"Did you talk to Eric?" It was Black Chuck.

"No, why?"

"It all went so wrong. They had a deal today. A big one. They got busted." He was talking a mile a minute.

"Busted? Who?"

"Scrap, Clyde, Karl, Max. Even Latoya. I can't believe this!"

"Are you sure? Did Scrap call you?"

"Homies across the street told me. They saw it all go down. And Julia, they said Eric was there too."

"Eric? He couldn't have been there. He's got the flu."

"Nah, Julia, he must've made that up. Guess he didn't want you to know he was part of the deal."

"I don't believe it." Eric wouldn't have cut out of an NFL game for a drug deal. He would never risk dealing in the first place.

"You better believe it. Raoul, Tariq, and Josh all saw him."

"Maybe it was somebody else!"

"They know what Eric looks like, Ju. Shit, this is the worst thing that could've happened. They got caught with so much . . . They're fucked!"

"Did you know about this deal, Chuck?"

"Yeah."

Tears blurred my vision. "This is a nightmare."

"For both of us."

I didn't sleep that night. I called Eric's cell again and again, hoping he'd answer and tell me everything was okay, but his phone was off.

It had to be a mistake. It couldn't have been Eric those guys saw hustled into a cop car with the lieutenants.

I slammed down the phone. If only I could get through! But I didn't have a home phone number for him—he'd always told me I could catch him on his cell.

I'd look up his number in the phone book! His dad's name was Arturo Valienté, and his crib was on Fourth Avenue. That was more than enough information.

I flipped through the Brooklyn White Pages. Valens, Valesquez . . . Valienté!

But no Arturo. No "A. Valienté" either.

Nothing.

I went to the Internet and googled the name Arturo Valienté on the off-chance that I'd find contact details.

Nothing. Nada.

I glanced at the clock. 4:17 a.m. It would be hours until I knew for sure if Eric had been arrested.

I crawled into bed, hugging my pillow. Tears welled up in my eyes.

Eric hadn't always told me everything, but I couldn't

imagine he would lie to me. That wasn't the guy I knew. My Eric told me the truth, even if it was hard to hear.

But if it *was* Eric who'd been arrested—then what?

Then he was a liar.

Then he'd be locked up for a long time.

ПOWHERE

"I need to know where he is!" It was the next morning, 11:35 a.m. I pleaded with the cop at Precinct 17. "He's my boyfriend and I'm really worried about him."

"Sorry, miss. I can't release that information."

Black Chuck banged his fist on the desk. "C'mon, man, tell my homegirl where he's at. Can't you see how torn up she is?"

"I can see that, Mr . . ."

"Black Chuck."

The cop frowned. "I can see that, er, Black Chuck. But I'm afraid she'll have to wait for her boyfriend to contact her. There's nothing I can do." He retreated to the inner office.

I plunked down in a chair. "I don't get it. How come you

heard from Scrap, and Jazz heard from Clyde, but I didn't hear from Eric?"

"I don't know. I'm sure he'll call you by the end of the day. He's probably meeting with a lawyer. Scrap did, first thing this morning, but he already had a lawyer. So maybe Eric don't have one yet."

"Maybe."

"Don't worry. You'll hear from him. And when you do, don't dog him out for lying to you, okay? He knows he done wrong. Tell him you love him and all that sweet shit. That's what he needs to hear."

"You're a sensitive guy, Chuck. I didn't know that about you."

"Yeah, well."

We sat there for a while, our elbows on our knees, our heads hanging down.

"How does it look for them?" I asked.

"Nobody's talking. Yet. But I bet the po-po will try to cut a deal with Latoya. You know, innocent woman caught in the middle."

"Do you think she'll go for it?"

"She'd be stupid not to."

"How long do you think . . ." I couldn't finish. The thought of Eric in jail boggled my mind.

"If you get caught with more than two ounces you get ten years."

"How do you know that?"

"Everybody knows that."

"You think they'll all go to jail?"

"No doubt. That's where most of us will end up sooner or later."

"What do you mean?"

He glanced at me. "You can't gangbang and stay square, Innocent."

"That's so cynical. What, have you been hustling too?"

"Here and there."

"But I thought you stayed out of that!"

"You either play the game or you don't. It ain't like you become a Crip and say, I'll do this, this, and this, and not that, and definitely not that, 'cause I don't wanna get put away. It don't work like that. I'll tell you something, Julia. It's by the grace of God that I wasn't there last night."

That pissed me off. "What are you saying? That God chose you over Eric? That you weren't meant to get caught, but that Eric and the rest of them were? That's bullshit. You got lucky."

Damn it, I was angry. Angry that Chuck was stupid

enough to get involved in the hustling game. Angry that he was free and Eric wasn't.

"You're right, Julia. I shouldn't have said it that way. I got nothing to be thanking the Lord for, especially now that Scrap is going down. He's all the family I got. Now I got nothing."

My heart broke for him. I wrapped my arms around him and hugged him tight, wishing I could protect him from the world.

"You got me, Chuck," I whispered. "It isn't much, but there it is."

ⵅARC

That afternoon I got a call from a number I didn't recognize. My heart jumped.

"Eric?"

"No, it's Black Chuck," he snapped. "You been talking to Eric?"

"No. You?"

"C'mon, Ju. Don't play me. I know Eric's out. He must've called you."

"Eric's *out*? Are you sure?"

"Guess he didn't want you to know he's a fucking narc. Set up his own brothers. Probably got a cut of the bust, tax-free. If I get my hands on Eric, I'm gonna end him!"

"Back up, back up. Maybe his dad bailed him out."

"Nobody had a bail hearing yet. Po-po let Eric walk right outta there."

"Seriously?" My heart leaped. Was Eric getting out of this somehow? Oh, God, please . . .

"When you talk to Eric, tell him to watch his back."

"I'm not gonna do that. Eric would never rat out his friends."

"He did a lot more than that, Ju. He's been working with the cops."

"You're crazy."

"Think about it: Less than two months after he joins the gang, we get raided *right after* a drop-off. The timing was too good—there had to be a snitch. And then Eric walks out with no charges!"

"I know it looks bad, but there's gotta be an explanation. I know Eric. He's loyal."

"You're blind, Ju. You're the one who told me he faked being sick so he could get in on the deal."

I didn't know what to say. He was right. Eric *had* lied to me.

Yeah, but lying was one thing—snitching was another. I just couldn't believe he would do it.

"I gotta go," Black Chuck said quickly. "It's my chance to

see Scrap. They got him behind glass. Behind glass!"

"Chuck . . . I'm so sorry."

"What are you sorry for? You got your boyfriend back. I bet he got rich off the deal."

"Shut the fuck up!" I slammed down the phone.

I stared at the wall.

Eric.

A narc.

A snitch.

It was impossible.

The cops must've had a reason for not charging him. They obviously realized that he wasn't one of the main players. Maybe he was just the first to get a bail hearing and the others didn't hear about it.

But I could see how the guys would think he could be a narc. People were always suspicious of the new guy. That didn't make it true though. Narcs were street scum. They cut deals with cops for their own benefit. Sold people out. That wasn't Eric. He was loyal.

But loyal to whom?

I remembered the tattoo.

Oh my God.

Was he a Latin King?

If he was, it made perfect sense. The Latin Kings and the FJC hated one another. Did Eric infiltrate the Crips so he could bring them down?

If it was true, it was genius.

Traitor

News that Eric might have snitched on the gang traveled fast. The next day at school, everybody stared at me, pointed, whispered.

I didn't have to go looking for the Crip girls. I knew they'd find me.

I just didn't know what they would do.

They came up to me two minutes after I got to my locker.

My pulse kicked up. Shutting my locker, I said, "Hey."

My split-second take was that they weren't going to attack me. Not this minute anyway. They all had books in their arms, and Sarah and Jazz carried brown-bagged breakfasts with grease spots on the bottom.

But their eyes had blades.

"What the fuck is going on, Julia?" Nessa demanded. "We heard your man ratted out Scrap and the lieutenants."

"I don't get it either. I haven't heard from Eric. I don't know why the cops let him go."

They exchanged looks. *Yeah, right.*

"It's true!" I said. "If Eric is . . . what everybody thinks he is, then I'm angry too. Then it means I never really knew him." I looked from one face to another, but I wasn't getting anywhere. "I had nothing to do with it."

"You joined right after he did," Apple Jax pointed out. "Pretty convenient, when you think about it."

I turned to Jazz, who stood there clutching her books, eerily quiet. "You believe me, right?"

Her eyes watered, but there was coldness behind them. "I don't know."

"Are you in some kind of trouble, Julia?" Sarah leaned forward, her chest inches from mine. "Is that why you did it? Did you cut a deal to save your ass?"

"Bullshit, I didn't cut any sort of deal. I don't have a record."

Nessa grinned nasty. "If that's true, it looks like your man left you behind. Nobody's seen Eric since he got out. He's probably out of state by now. Unless . . . he's staying with you."

"I told you, I haven't seen him." It hit me that she may be right—Eric might've left town. Would I ever see him again? Would I ever find out what really happened?

It was unbearable. I felt sick.

Sarah pouted. "Aw, look, poor Julia's upset that her boo ran off on her."

They snickered.

I stalked off, half expecting them to follow me, half hoping they would.

I guess they were in no rush. There was always after school.

Eric, where the hell are you?

What did you do?

How could you have left me in the middle of this?

The minutes ticked by slowly. I sat in my classes, drowning in my thoughts, wishing I could disappear.

It didn't matter that I was innocent. The Crips saw me as guilty by association, and one way or another, they were going to make me pay for what they thought Eric had done.

At lunch I sat at my locker, alone and jittery. I chewed some food without tasting it. Every time somebody passed me, I looked up to make sure they weren't going to pounce.

I recognized Q's shoes coming up to me. It was a relief to see her. And it looked like she was actually going to talk to me.

"Are you okay?" she asked.

I shrugged.

"Is it true what they're saying about Eric?"

She hadn't talked to me at school in ages, and *this* was what she wanted to talk about? I shouldn't have been surprised.

I looked up at her. "What do you care?"

"I always cared."

I patted the cold linoleum floor beside me. "Wanna have lunch, then?"

"Uh, I already ate."

I snorted. What did I expect? She just wanted the gossip to bring back to the girls. "I got nothing for you."

"Well, okay. See you later." She hurried off.

Fuck you, too, I thought, and balled up my lunch.

"Going home?"

Black Chuck popped up by my locker after the last bell. I hadn't even thought he was at school today.

"Yeah. You?"

He nodded.

"Great." I zipped up my coat and slung my book bag over my shoulder. "Let's go."

Outside, I took a breath of cold air and let it blast through my lungs. Relief. I was going to make it home today. Nobody would touch me if I was with Black Chuck.

I glanced at him. "Don't wanna see me get jumped, eh?"

He didn't smile. "No."

"Do you plan to escort me to and from school every day?" I asked.

"Until everybody calms down, I just might do that." His eyes were serious. "I'm sorry for how I acted on the phone. I know you had no clue what Eric was doing."

I nodded, hot tears flooding my eyes.

He put his arm around me. "I'm trying to get the gang to chill. They don't know you like I do. Don't worry, Ju. I won't let them touch you."

"Th-thanks."

"They'll see the truth eventually. They're all riled up right now and looking for someone to blame."

We got on the bus in front of the school, grabbed a seat near the front. I was so thankful to have Black Chuck with me. He was a true friend, maybe the only one I'd ever had.

We didn't talk as the bus made its stops. I'd never seen Black Chuck so depressed, not even with all the drama with his mom over the years. Losing Scrap had really taken something out of him.

My cell phone buzzed in my coat pocket. I flicked it open.

MEET ME IN PROSPECT PARK @ 4 ENTRANCE NEAR LIBRARY. DONT TELL ANYBODY. E.

Oh my God.

I quickly closed my phone, glancing at Black Chuck. He was staring out the window, in his own world.

"So we gonna get burgers or what?" he said.

"Later, yeah. Dad just texted me a grocery list. I'll meet you at the A-raab place at six."

"A'ight," he said, his eyes still fixated on the window.

PAYBACK

It was time to learn the truth.

I sat on the steps of the library, hugging myself against the cold. I was desperate to see him, but terrified of what he might tell me. I wanted him to be innocent of everything, but it didn't seem possible.

"Divine."

I looked up. Eric's hair was messed up by the wind. His dark eyes were soft. He was dressed different than usual—the blue jeans were tighter, the jacket was wool, the black sweater underneath was almost preppy.

I got up. "Hey."

"Hey." He didn't come closer.

"What's going on, Eric?"

"Walk with me."

We headed into Prospect Park. It was deserted today, cold and gloomy. The trees were dead and the ground was almost frozen, but there was no snow to bring out the kids.

I waited for him to start. Once we were walking down a path through trees, he did.

"My name's Eric, but my last name isn't Valienté. I'm not from Detroit. I'm from Bay Ridge."

"You're from Brooklyn?"

"Born and raised. It's where I fucked up my life. I joined the Latin Kings when I was fourteen."

"And I believed your story about the tattoo. I'm such an idiot."

"It was a good lie, Julia. My lies had to be good if I was gonna do what I had to do. Don't blame yourself for buying it. Everybody did. Even Darnell."

"Who?"

"Scrap. I don't use gang names anymore. Not since I left the Kings."

"So you're not a spy for the Kings?"

"No, I left a couple of years ago. I was sick of living that way, sick of being in and out of juvey. I wanted to turn my life around, and I did. But last year the cops caught me with weed—enough that they could charge me with dealing. They were gonna try me as an adult because I was eighteen, but they offered me a deal to reduce my sentence. They needed a kid to infiltrate the Flatbush Junction Crips."

"Black Chuck was right about you."

"Yeah, well, the cops gave me a chance to put away Darnell Charles. I wasn't gonna pass that up."

"But you didn't know him, did you? Why would you want to put him away?"

"Because of my brother." His face hardened. "He was just a kid, running with the Kings, dealing where he shouldn't have been. Darnell could've just scared him off. Instead he stabbed him and left him to die." His eyes had the same dark intensity they'd had the first time he'd mentioned his brother. "There were witnesses—Crips, bystanders. The whole neighborhood knew who did it, but everybody was too afraid to talk to the cops."

"That's horrible."

"I told you that joining the gang was for my brother. It was true."

I nodded, my throat feeling tight.

He stared at the paved path. "I know you're wondering how you fit into all this. I owe you an explanation for that too. Approaching the Crips on the street wasn't gonna work. I needed to find another way in. Cops thought I should go through Black Chuck. We figured the best way to get to him was through you."

I felt something inside me crack and splinter. Eric had been using me the whole time. And I'd made it so easy for him, falling for him right away, giving him the perfect chance to get close to Chuck.

But one thing didn't make sense. "Why did you want to get back together after we broke up, then? You were in already, weren't you?"

"Yeah. Getting back together was probably a mistake. I told myself it made a better cover—that it would look too convenient if we broke up right after I joined the gang. But . . . that isn't the real reason I did it." He glanced at me. "I never meant to start liking you."

"So you're saying it wasn't *all* an act," I said.

"Right." His jaw was tight and he tried not to look at me. I didn't know if he was telling me the truth or just what he thought I wanted to hear.

"What about when I joined the gang?" I asked. "Did that help your plan?"

"If anything, it fucked with it. I didn't want you to join. I never thought you would."

I said nothing. I'd never thought I would either.

He looked me dead in the eye. "You have to get out, Julia."

"That's not your problem."

"You're not listening to me."

"Yeah, I am. Maybe I *want* to get out. Can you tell me how? They want to jump me anyway, because they think I had something to do with what you did. If I ask them to jump me out, I'll get seriously fucked."

"That's exactly why you have to get out. Trust me, staying in will fuck up your life. Find a way. Get your dad to move. Go live with relatives in another city. Do whatever you gotta do. You know what I found out about gangs, Julia? It's always the same deal. Once you sign up, you're nothing more than a bitch taking orders. You think you got power, you got nothing. I am done with it, Julia. I am so fucking done."

I wished I was done too.

But I knew I was trapped.

"I'll try to get out," I mumbled. Whatever *try* meant. "I'd better go. You're not even supposed to be talking to me."

"I couldn't leave without telling you the truth."

"You're leaving Brooklyn?"

"Tonight. My mom is already living in—"

"Don't. Don't tell me anything the cops don't want me to know."

"But *I* want you to know. I'm moving to Miami. Most of my family's from down there. I'm gonna study culinary management."

"That part was real."

"Other parts too." His eyes burned into me. "It doesn't have to be over."

I tore my eyes away. How could it not be over? How could I ever trust him again? He'd lied to everybody. He'd done it to reduce his own sentence and to avenge his brother. But who would save Jazz's brother, Clyde? Or the other lieutenants who'd been arrested? Didn't they deserve a second chance too?

But that was the thing about the game. It wasn't fair. Eric knew that better than anyone. He'd taken the deal, avenged his brother, and earned himself another life. Shouldn't I give him props for that?

"I don't expect you to make any decisions right away," he said. "If you want to contact me, this is how." He handed me a folded piece of paper. "This has my real name and my info in Miami. It's up to you. Even if you just want to call and ask me more questions, I'll answer them. No strings."

"You shouldn't give me this."

"Memorize it if you have to. I trust you to keep me safe. Good-bye, Julia."

He hugged me. I stood there, stiff, not letting myself hug him back.

I didn't want to let him walk away, but I didn't know what else to do. Should I tell him I forgave him when I wasn't sure if I did? All I knew was that, whoever he was, I didn't want him to go.

And then, in the bushes, I saw a flash of blue.

"Eric!"

He didn't see the two guys in blue ski masks until they were on top of him.

It all happened so fast. Eric got a punch in the face, then in the stomach. He stumbled back, dodging the next one, then came back fiercely, launching his weight at one of the guys, knocking him off his feet. Eric smashed a kick into the guy's side, but the other attacker put him in a choke hold, dragging him to the ground. Eric struggled like a maniac, but the guy on the ground got on top of him, digging his knees into his chest.

I didn't think. I ran up, fumbling in my pocket for my pepper spray, popping off the cap. The Crips weren't paying attention to what I was doing—they were focused on keeping

Eric pinned. I ran up beside them, pointed my pepper spray right into the face of the guy on Eric's chest, and let it fly. He fell back, bawling, throwing a hand over his eyes. I didn't see the switchblade until he lashed out.

I fell back, losing my focus, losing my legs.

"The fuck did you do?" one of the ski masks screamed.

I knew that voice.

They scrambled to their feet and ran. I was on the ground, pressing my hands to the pain, feeling my gloves get wet, soaking up blood like a sponge.

"Oh God. Oh God." I saw Eric above me, the bottom half of his face covered in blood. *He'll be okay*, I thought, somewhere in the fog. Probably just a broken nose.

As for me . . .

He took off his jacket and pressed it against my stomach. Hot pain flashed through me. My scream came out like a groan.

Black spots clouded my vision. Or maybe it was his blood dripping into my face.

Part of the pressure lifted off my stomach. I twisted in agony, glimpsed his shaky hand fumbling with his cell.

911. He was calling 911.

". . . Prospect . . . hurry . . . it won't stop!"

Cold. I was so cold. Shivering uncontrollably. I started to slide.

"Julia stay with me!" he shouted. But he sounded miles away now, across a void I couldn't cross.

And I was going under.

LIFELINE

I WANTED TO STAY WITH U. THEY MADE ME GO. THEY DRAGGED ME AWAY FROM U. THEY TOLD ME IF I DIDNT GET ON A PLANE THEYD LOCK ME UP FOR MY OWN PROTECTION. I CALLED THE HOSPITAL EVERY DAY. THEY WOULDNT TELL ME ANYTHING ABOUT U OR EVEN IF U WERE STILL AT THIS HOSPITAL. FINALLY THEY LET ME TALK TO UR DAD. HE DOESNT KNOW WHY THIS HAPPENED. I DIDNT TELL HIM ANYTHING. HE TOLD ME UD BE RESTING FOR A WHILE. HE TOLD ME HED GIVE U UR CELL WHEN U WOKE UP SO U COULD READ THIS. PLEASE LET ME KNOW WHEN YOU WAKE UP. I NEED TO KNOW UR OK. PLEASE. LOVE, ERIC.

I looked at my dad, who was sitting beside the bed. He looked like hell, unshaven, dark circles under his eyes. I wasn't sure how long he'd been here or how many days I'd been here. I was groggy from the drugs and wondered if I could float the hell out of here.

"I thought hearing from Eric might cheer you up." He searched my eyes. "Can I ask what happened?"

"I don't want to talk about it." I wasn't sure what to do with what I knew, but until I figured it out, I had to keep my mouth shut. I shifted a little in the bed, feeling a dull ache in my abdomen, remembering when it felt like fire. "When am I getting out of here?"

"Probably a few more days."

"How many stitches did I get?"

"I'm not sure." His dark eyes were sad. "Your liver ruptured, Julia. You're going to be laid up for a while."

I wasn't sure what a ruptured liver meant, but it terrified me. I wished I hadn't asked.

"But I will get better, right?"

"Yes."

I hoped he was telling me the truth. I knew that when you're sick, people tell you what you want to hear.

I looked back down at the cell, pressing reply to Eric's message:

I MISS U SO MUCH.

NO REWIND

The hospital was wack, but drugs kept me dreamy. When I got home, they eased up on my drugs, which made the pain worse and killed my buzz.

For the few first days, my dad stayed home, but then he had to go back to work. I was all alone with my thoughts and a darkness that could swallow me.

I didn't know what I would've done without my poetry. When you're laid up and want to cry but don't want to bust your stomach open, you have to find some way of venting your feelings. I filled up a whole notebook with poems. I even sent one in to the poetry contest, determined to win that fifty bucks.

Q called twice. I didn't answer the phone. Of course she

would call—it was the *right* thing to do. Q always did the right thing. We didn't have that in common, did we?

Truth was, we didn't have anything in common anymore. All we had was the past.

I was done pretending. It was time to be real.

I decided to do her a favor and not return her calls.

Black Chuck called too, I guess to make sure I wasn't dead. I didn't answer his calls either.

At least I had my dad. He didn't drop the ball on me. He actually hung out with me when he wasn't working. I'd never watched so much ESPN in my life, but it was cool having him around. He even started inviting Gina over to chill with us. Sometimes she stopped in when he wasn't there, just to chat or cook for me. Turned out she wasn't half bad.

And besides my dad, I had a lifeline. A lifeline I talked to on the phone every single night. His name was Eric Vargas, not Valienté.

He was a snitch, the most notorious one in Brooklyn right now.

He was the guy who brought down Scrap and the lieutenants of the FJC and then disappeared. Yeah, he was a snitch, and I loved him.

"I've been stalling on giving a statement to the cops," I told Eric one night on the phone. "I said I wasn't feeling well enough yet. They know I'm full of shit." I sighed. "It would've been easier if you'd just told them who jumped us."

"I didn't know a hundred percent who they were until you told me, Julia. This is your call, not mine."

"But I don't know what to do!"

"Your safety has to be your number-one concern. Do you think the Crips will come after you if you talk?"

"I think they'll come after me anyway. They blame me for letting you infiltrate. I'm sure they see the fact that I met with you that day as proof."

"If you think they'll come after you anyway, why are you stalling on telling the cops?"

"Because . . . you *know* why. I don't want Chuck to go to jail. But Rolo—I'd love to see him go down. Who knows what he might've done to you with that blade?"

"I don't give a shit about that. It's what he did to you that kills me."

"I'm pretty sure what happened to me wasn't part of their plan."

"It wasn't part of Black Chuck's plan, that's for sure. But Rolo? I don't know. I always had a bad feeling about him."

I paused, thinking.

"Julia?"

"I know what I have to do."

"Oh yeah?"

"I'm going to use what I know to bargain with them. Think about it, Eric. Knowing who stabbed me can buy me protection. It can be my bargaining chip to keep them from coming after me."

"You're talking about blackmailing the Crips," he said.

"Exactly. I think it can work."

"I like how you think, Julia."

"That's because I think like you."

The next day Dad brought me a cup of herbal tea and cookies. He was softening me up for something, I just didn't know what. I could tell by the look on his face that he was going to say something big.

Poor Dad was still traumatized by what happened to me, and he didn't know the half of it. He thought the attack on Eric and me was a random mugging turned bloody.

I couldn't tell him the truth. No way could I come clean about my involvement with the Crips. No way could I tell him Eric's role in all of this. He'd never trust me again if he knew what I did. And he'd never accept Eric if he knew his past.

"What's up, Dad? You and Gina getting married or something?"

He looked startled, then laughed. "It isn't that, trust me."

"It's not a bad idea," I said. "So what is it, then?"

He sat down in the recliner across from me. "Gina's niece goes to a really good school up in Washington Heights. We went yesterday to check it out. I think it would be a good place for you."

"It's a Catholic school?"

"Yeah, but it's not run by nuns or anything. It's a good, quality type of place, and it's a place I can afford to send you. I was thinking that when you're up to it, Gina and I would take you to check it out."

"Don't bother. Just sign me up."

He looked stunned. "You'll go for it?"

"Yeah."

"Great! You'd have to go for an interview, but I'm sure you won't have any problems getting in. And there's one more thing. I thought since you'll be going to school up there, it would make sense if we move."

"To the city?"

"To Queens. I want you out of this neighborhood. I won't be able to sleep at night if you're still on these streets. I hope you feel good about moving, Julia, but I'm not leaving you any choice in this. I've already given the landlord notice."

I took a deep breath. So many things changing at the same time. But it had to be right. There was no going back. No rewind button on the past few months.

"I'm cool with that too," I said.

THE VISITOR

He buzzed the crib. Wasn't like him to be on time.

I trudged over to the door, pressing the button. Then I went back to the couch and put my feet up.

He knocked.

"Come in!"

Black Chuck came in, taking off his blue do-rag and stuffing it into his jacket pocket. "Hey."

"Hi, Chuck."

He sat down across from me. "How you feeling?"

"Good, as long as I don't need my liver to work anytime soon."

"Shit." He fidgeted with his hands. "You never returned my calls."

"You weren't surprised, eh, Chuck?"

He didn't say anything. What could he say?

I wasn't sure where to start. "How's Jazz doing?"

"Getting by. Her grandma didn't kick her out."

"That's good. How's Rolo?" Maybe I didn't need to ask that. Maybe I just wanted to watch him squirm.

"Rolo took over for Scrap as head."

"Did he? I thought maybe you would."

"Nah, I ain't a leader. Anyway, everybody will welcome you back when you're ready."

"You've gotta be kidding me. They all think I knew about Eric's plan."

"You still officially Crip, Julia. You a member for life."

"That's what I wanted to talk to you about. I know Crips have this thing about jumping people out. I want you to tell the others that when I got stabbed *that* was like being jumped out."

"I think . . . they might go for it."

"They will, once you tell them you and Rolo took care of me personally."

He stilled. "I don't know what you mean."

"I always trusted you, Chuck. Don't wreck that. I recognized your voice. You and Rolo should be locked up right now. But I covered for you."

He looked down at his knees. "Why?"

"Because I want this to end. And I know why you went after Eric. I don't blame you for wanting to jump him. But Rolo meant to slash him up."

"I didn't know Rolo was planning to do that. That's the honest truth, Julia."

"It doesn't matter now. You never figured it out, did you?"

"Figured what out?"

"That Eric didn't sell you out. He protected you. Who do you think told me to invite you to the game that night? Whose tickets did we use?"

"*What?*"

"You knew they were Eric's tickets. It never occurred to you that maybe he wanted you at that game because he wanted you out of the way during the bust?"

Black Chuck blinked. "He *told* you to invite me?"

"Yeah. I wanted to take Jazz, but he said it should be you."

"Why?"

"Because you were friends. Maybe he wanted to give you a chance to walk away from the Crips."

Bitterness flared in his eyes. "I'm supposed to thank him for letting me off when he set up my homies and my brother?"

"You're not supposed to thank him."

"Why the fuck did he set them up, Julia?"

"I can't tell you why, but he had reasons. I bet you would've done the same thing."

"Not me. I would never snitch, not even to save my own ass. That *is* why he did it, right?"

"It's not that simple, Chuck. That's all I'm saying."

"You still talking to him, aren't you?"

"I wouldn't tell you if I was, Chuck."

"Forget I asked."

"Forgotten."

He was quiet for a long time. I knew he didn't want to take his anger out on me. I knew that he was probably the only Crip who didn't think I'd been a part of Eric's scheme. He knew me too well for that.

"So . . . are you coming back to school soon?" he asked.

"I'm not coming back ever. I'm moving."

"Moving? You don't have to do that, Ju. I'll tell the gang that you got jumped out. Nobody will come after you."

"Thanks, Chuck. You do that. Because I could run into the Crips anytime, and I need to know that they'll stay away from me."

"No worries, Ju."

"Good. I want you to put it to them this way—if anybody comes after me, I'll tell the cops it was you and Rolo who attacked us. You have to make that clear to them if I'm gonna be safe. Their new head will *go down* if I get hurt. Promise me you'll make it clear."

"I will."

"Thanks." I sighed. "I have a chance to start over, and I'm gonna take it. I wish you would too."

Silence pressed down on us. I didn't even know why I'd bothered to say it. There was no way he was going to leave the gang.

"I'm sorry, Julia." He got to his feet.

I couldn't look at him. I loved him like a brother, and I forgave him for what he'd done—but I knew we couldn't be friends anymore. It was too risky. If any of the Crips found out that we were still in touch, they might use him to get to me or Eric. So I had to disappear.

We'd both made our choices.

"Bye, Black Chuck."

The Letter

I found a letter on the kitchen table addressed to me. The sender's address was South Bay High School. I tore it open.

Dear Julia,

Exciting news—you won the poetry contest! Your poem was published in the *Bay Times*. We all want to congratulate you and wish you the best of luck at your new school.

Sincerely,
Mr. Britt and the South Bay Writing Club

The check dropped out of the envelope.

Fifty bucks.

It would go straight into the bank.

Because I had an open invitation to visit Miami.

Allison van Diepen is a high school social studies teacher who is often mistaken for a student. She spent three and a half years teaching at one of Brooklyn's most dangerous public high schools. She now teaches at an alternative school in her hometown of Ottawa, Canada. Visit her on the Web at www.allisonvandiepen.com.